ALSO BY MEARA PLATT

EARL OF
Westcliff

MEARA
PLATT

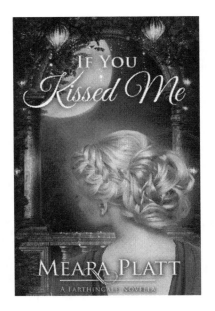

**Sign up for Meara Platt's newsletter
and you'll receive a free, exclusive copy**
of her Farthingale novella,
If You Kissed Me.

Visit her website
to grab your free copy:
mearaplatt.com

CHAPTER ONE

Wicked Earls' Club, London
October 1815

TYNAN BRAYDEN, THE sixth Earl of Westcliff, peered out of the window of his club onto Bedford Place, knowing he had a choice to make – either remove the last of his clothing and join the beautiful viscountess who was already naked in his bed, eager to share a night of pleasure with him – or leave his private bedchamber to discover the identity of the young woman draped in moonlight who was standing alone across the street from his club for the third night in a row and find out what she was doing there.

Was there a doubt of his decision?

He eyed the strawberries and cream, the peacock feather, and the black silk ribbons sitting atop his bureau and sighed. "We'll have to do this another night, Daniella. Something has just come up." He intended no pun by his remark, nor was the viscountess clever enough to understand the double meaning in his words.

"Is it my husband?" Daniella, Lady Bascom, leaped from his bed and hastily tossed on her elegant silk gown. "He must have returned to London early. Or never left at all. Why, that deceitful liar! He must have hired Bow Street runners to follow me." She gathered up the undergarments she'd removed moments earlier and fled from his room without giving him so much as a passing glance.

"Have a good evening," Tynan muttered as she slammed the door behind her. In truth, he was relieved. Their nights, despite the sex games she often enjoyed playing, had grown quite dull and unsatisfying to him. Intimacy, he supposed, required the participating parties to actually feel something for each other. Something more than indifference.

He returned his attention to the young lady who stood alone on the street, no sign of her driver or carriage this evening, which left her easy prey for any passerby who wished to take advantage. Out there, she was vulnerable. A lost rabbit among a pack of wolves.

"Bollocks." Three of those wolves had just spotted her and were now about to circle her.

He grabbed his boots, quickly stuffing his feet into them, and at the same time glancing around for the shirt he'd removed only moments ago. Daniella, he realized, must have scooped it up along with her undergarments in her mad rush to flee his chamber. There was no time to grab another, for those three not so fine gentlemen were dangerously close to his little rabbit, eyeing her for their next meal. *His little rabbit?* No, he didn't know the girl and had no intention of getting involved beyond rescuing her from this scrape.

Tynan knew he had to move fast. By the sidelong glances these men were casting her, and their sudden whispers to each other, they were about to make their move.

He reached for his pistols and hurried downstairs, hoping to make it out of the club and across the street before the girl was harmed. Not that he should care or feel protective of her in any way. Or that he should still nonsensically be thinking of her as *his* little rabbit. Where was her family? Did no one notice her missing?

There was a chill to the air on this October evening, a hint of upcoming winter. Tynan felt the wind's cool prickle against his chest the moment he stepped out of his club. "You there... girl." He didn't know what to call her. My darling bunny was not at all appropriate. Was she married? A spinster? No, she looked too young to be on the shelf. But not too young to know better than to be traipsing about London alone at night. "Get behind me."

She frowned at him. "Do I know you, sir?"

"No, nor do I believe you know those three gentlemen who are eyeing you for dessert." He turned to the three obviously inebriated men and trained his pistols on them. "Take another step toward the girl and it shall be your last."

"No need for that, m'lord," said their leader, an arrogant fellow with a cruel smile and an avid gleam in his eyes that revealed his less than honorable intentions toward the girl. He had no business here. Not that this was one of the finer London neighborhoods, but neither was it anywhere near the worst. The townhouses on Bedford Place were neatly maintained and might have been considered elegant if not for their occupants who were mostly mistresses and courtesans who plied their trade to a fashionable clientele. "We're willin' to share her with you."

The girl scurried to Tynan's side. "I am indebted to you, sir. I hadn't noticed them. I'm glad you did."

Her voice was soft and lilting.

He caught the scent of roses on her skin, with a subtle hint of lemon and summer sunshine mixed in.

She was prettier than he'd expected, but he dared not take his gaze off the blackguards, not while they were obviously mulling how best to overpower him and grab the girl. "Get inside," he ordered her. "You'll be safe with me. I give you my word of honor."

She hesitated.

"I have no wish to spill blood, but these gentlemen are determined to have you. I'll be forced to shoot them if you continue to stand here and provide temptation."

"Oh, I see." She stepped into the club.

He backed in after her, his gaze and pistols trained on the men who were not at all pleased that their little rabbit had just gotten away. He shoved the door closed and called for two passing footmen to stand guard. "Keep weapons at hand. We might have trouble from those drunken fools tonight."

They both nodded. "Aye, m'lord."

"Has Lord Coventry arrived yet? Or Sussex or Wainthorpe?"

"No, m'lord," the older footman said. "Nor any of the other earls."

"When they do arrive, warn them to remain alert." He waited for these trusted retainers to take their positions by the door, and then turned scowling toward the girl. "Are you attics to let? Where is your driver? More important, why have you been standing across the street, scouting this building for the past three nights?"

When she did not deign to respond, he tucked the smaller pistol into its holster in his boot, grabbed her hand, and attempted to haul her upstairs to his quarters. She stood her ground and fought back, determined to shove away from him. "Unhand me!"

"Not until I have my answers." Having no patience for her resistance, he lifted her over his shoulder.

She gasped and pounded on his back. "You gave me your word of honor! Where are you taking me?"

"Somewhere we can continue this discussion in private." He did not particularly care who saw her, but the lords and ladies who frequented the

Wicked Earls' Club expected discretion and could not afford to be seen by her... whoever she was.

He marched into his chamber and shut the door behind them, ignoring her startled cry as the latch fell into place. He set her down in the center of the room and moved away, for she was obviously scared of him and he needed to calm her down. "What is your business here?"

"You wretch!"

He growled when she unexpectedly kicked his shin and tried to dodge around him to reach the door.

He grabbed her by the waist and drew her up against him, his intention merely to prevent her escape. To his surprise, she felt soft and wonderful. He released her, but made certain to stand between her and the door. "Why did you kick me?"

Instead of replying, she fumbled through her reticule and withdrew her own pistol. With a small, trembling hand, she pointed it at him. "You assured me that I would be safe with you."

"Put that thing down before you hurt yourself." He moved toward his desk and set his own pistol down on it. "You are safe with me. I have no interest in making you my next bed partner." Although he'd just gotten a good look at the girl and – *holy hell* – she was beautiful. Auburn hair that was lush and silky, and hinting of curls that were too unruly to ever properly behave. Big amber-brown eyes that were the vibrant color of expensive brandy. And a body that had his heart pounding so hard, it almost dropped him to his knees.

He doubted that she trusted him, and in this moment, he wasn't certain that he could be trusted with her.

Her lips were tantalizingly soft and pink. He'd been too busy staring at them to realize she'd lowered her weapon. "I may as well introduce myself. Tynan Brayden, Earl of Westcliff, at your service."

Her lips puckered as he gave a mock bow. "An earl," she said, placing emphasis on his title. "My goodness."

He arched an eyebrow, relieved when she finally stuck the pistol back in her reticule. He noted that her hands were still trembling. "Your turn," he said, purposely keeping his voice gentle. "Who are you?"

"No one of consequence, I assure you. Miss Abigail Croft. My brother is Peter Croft, Baron Whitpool. His is an old title, but that's about all that can be said for the good. In truth, I feel it is more of a family curse."

He could hear the heartbreak in her every word.

"I wasn't here because of your club." Her release of breath came out in a ragged and rather forlorn sigh. "I was trying to work up the courage to enter the house next door. It is where my brother goes nightly... for his... to forget about the demons that haunt him."

Any irritation he might have felt toward the girl's folly had now fled. If Tynan understood her correctly, her brother was an addict. Bollocks, that was trouble. He and his fellow earls had become increasingly concerned by the fashionable artists salon next door that had lately turned into something more sinister. The place was frequented by romantic poets, many of whom were darlings of the *ton*. Someone in very high authority shielded them, perhaps not realizing this house was more of an opium den than a salon for patrons of enlightened literature. "I'm truly sorry, Miss Croft. How long has this been going on with your brother?"

"Ever since he returned home from the war. He was recalled from his regiment when he came into the title last year. But his condition has gotten especially bad these past few months. Perhaps he's been like this for years and I hadn't noticed until now. He was wounded years ago in Spain fighting Napoleon's forces, you see."

Tynan regarded her with concern. "He was a soldier?"

She clasped her hands together, wringing them as she nodded. "The youngest of four sons, so it was either fighting or the clergy for him. He chose fighting." She cast Tynan a wincing smile. "I love him, but Peter was never the pious sort. My parents knew it, too. As for me, I was the accidental fifth child, the girl they had hoped for and finally got. Being the only girl among all those boys, and the youngest as well, I was either picked on mercilessly or worshiped. There was never a middle ground."

If she had four older brothers, then where were the other three? Why was she left the task of bringing Peter home? It made no sense.

She cleared her throat. "My lord, have you lost your shirt?"

"What?" He glanced down, noting he was clad only in his trousers and boots, and only now recalling he'd run out in this state of undress. He kept a wardrobe at his club, but he'd been too distracted by the girl to bother making himself respectable. Was it necessary? She was in his chamber. Alone with him. They were strangers to each other. There was nothing respectable about their situation. "Give me a moment."

He fetched a clean shirt and slipped it on, buttoning it only part way up and rolling up his shirt sleeves since he wasn't going to fumble with cufflinks or don a bloody cravat, vest, or jacket for her sake. In truth, there was a sensual innocence about the girl that made him think of shedding clothes – mainly hers – rather than tediously putting his on.

Her gown was seductively prim, he noticed. A dark blue woolen weave with a white lace collar that buttoned to her throat. A man would have to work for hours to slip that gown off her slender shoulders. He ran his gaze up and down her body once more. Ah, but she'd be worth every bit of the effort it would take to peel those layers off her. "I'm afraid I cannot leave my club yet, Miss Croft. If you promise not to run off the moment my back is turned, I'll have my carriage brought around to take you home."

She nodded. "I give you my word. Thank you. This was my driver's night off and I foolishly thought... well, clearly, I wasn't thinking. I'd hired a hack and paid the driver to wait for me, but the horrid man disappeared the moment I handed over the money. I was stranded and didn't know what to do."

As though fully realizing just how incredibly idiotic and dangerous her actions had been, she blushed and glanced away.

Her innocent eyes lit up the moment she noticed what was sitting upon his bureau top. "Are those strawberries? And cream?"

Tynan realized she was hungry and not thinking of the games one played in bed with... never mind. "Yes, please have them. I'll ring for some more food to be brought up for you while you await your ride home."

"Oh, no. It isn't necessary. The strawberries are perfect. Thank you." She dipped one in cream, closed her eyes, and tipped her head back to take it into her mouth. Her tongue darted out to lick at a spot of cream that had landed at the corner of her mouth. "Oh, my. This is heavenly."

Holy hell.

Her eyes were still closed while she slowly savored each lush, juicy bite. "Would you care for one, my lord?"

"No, Miss Croft." His throat was suddenly as tight as the rest of his body. "Have them all. I wouldn't deny you the obvious pleasure."

She opened her eyes and smiled at him in appreciation, a genuinely sincere and warm smile that upended his heart once again.

"Oh, and what a lovely feather."

Bollocks.

"It's a peacock feather, isn't it?"

He wished the girl would keep her hands off those things. In truth, they weren't his. The viscountess had brought the peacock feather and silk bindings along in anticipation of a night of erotic fantasy. Her fantasies. Not his. He was merely her chosen stud bull.

Since he was single, unattached, and feeling particularly restless lately, he'd accepted her proposition. Meaningless sex with a beautiful woman who wanted no commitment.

So why was he relieved that it had not taken place?

Worse, why was he enjoying his night of celibacy with one of the most clueless young women ever to cross his path?

"Oh, what lovely silk ribbons. They're a rich, lustrous black. What are you–"

"Give me those." He grabbed them from her fingers and stuck them in the top drawer of his desk. "I gave you permission to eat my strawberries, not dig through my belongings."

Her eyes rounded in surprise. "The ribbons are yours?"

He cleared his throat that was still so tight, it was a miracle he didn't sound like a bullfrog. "They belong to a friend. None of your business who she is."

"I suppose the peacock feather is hers, too." She held it up against her hair, no doubt believing it was a hair adornment and not... never mind.

"Put that thing down. Where were you raised? In an isolated abbey in the wilds of Yorkshire? Did no one ever teach you manners?"

She glanced up at him in surprise. "Yes, my abbey was in Yorkshire. How did you know?"

He frowned. "But you just told me that you had a family. Four brothers. Parents."

She nodded, her expression suddenly turning pained. "My mother died when I was five. My father passed on shortly afterward. My eldest brother, Thomas, became Baron Whitpool. He tried to keep us all together, but couldn't manage us and the Whitpool properties, all of which were run down and plagued with debt. I was too young to help out, and my other three brothers were terrors even when under our parents' strict supervision."

She paused a moment and glanced around. "My lord, may I sit?"

"Of course. Forgive my rudeness."

However, before he had a chance to pull out the lone chair that was situated behind his writing desk, she sank onto his bed and released a breathy sigh. "Thomas married a girl from a wealthy, local family," she said, her slender shoulders sagging from the weight of her obvious unhappiness. "He hoped she would help him restore order to the Whitpool household. She did, by shipping me off to the abbey. I remained there until I was sixteen."

"How long ago was that?"

Her big, sad eyes met his stern gaze. "Are you asking me how old I am?"

He folded his arms across his chest, needing to do something to distract him from the heat flowing through his veins and the inexplicable urge to hold her in his arms and protect her forever. Perhaps he was the one who needed protection from her. He turned away and grabbed his vest, putting it on as he answered her question. The more layers between them, the better. "I just saved your life. I deserve some answers."

She nodded. "I suppose you do. I'm twenty years old. My brother, Thomas, died when I was sixteen. Childless. So his horrid ogre of a wife returned to her family and William became the new Baron Whitpool. He brought me back home. By then, he and our other brother, Gideon, had established a shipping company that hauled freight back and forth from the West Indies. Sugar. Spices. Rum."

"They must have been successful businessmen." He'd learned much in running the Westcliff properties as well as assisting to run this establishment. Even if one hired excellent managers, there was no substitute for one's own diligence and attentiveness.

"Yes, they were. William never gave up his love of the sea. Despite his baronial responsibilities, he often joined Gideon on the shorter trips, sometimes to Ireland and sometimes to Flanders. They were caught last year in a sudden squall off the Irish Sea." Her voice turned tremulous and raspy. "Both of my brothers drowned."

He didn't know what to say. So many losses in so short a span of time. He had three brothers of his own and could not imagine how he would have handled losing any of them. He felt a sudden pang of remorse. He hadn't seen his family in a while. Perhaps he would stop by his mother's townhouse for an overdue visit. Perhaps he'd invite this girl along when he did. "I'm so sorry, Abigail. Truly."

"Thank you, my lord."

"No, call me Tynan. Or just Ty." That's what his brothers called him when they weren't calling him something worse. They all loved each other, but they were brothers, after all. How else were they to show their love if not by mercilessly pounding on each other? "Call me whatever you wish."

He did not bother with formality.

She hadn't taken offense when he'd called her Abigail instead of Miss Croft. It felt right to do so. There was no propriety to their situation, especially not now with her sitting atop the silk sheets of his four-poster bed. He dragged the chair out from behind his desk and moved it near the bed. Turning it around, he rested his arms on its high back and sat straddling the seat so that he could face her.

The chair's high back served as a barrier between them.

A necessary barrier, for she'd somehow stripped away his irritation. All he wanted to do was take her in his arms and comfort her.

In truth, he wanted to do much more.

But he wasn't going to touch her. He'd promised.

She looked as soft and vulnerable as a gentle rabbit. *His little rabbit.* But he liked that she was also strong and spirited, ready to fight to save her last surviving brother. "Tell me more about Peter."

What he really wanted to know was more about her.

Every blessed thing he could learn about her.

She curled her hands around the bedpost, as though the sad memories had cast her adrift and she needed to hold onto something solid that would serve as her anchor. "There isn't much more to tell. He came home to take over the title and its responsibilities, but he'd been wounded during his military service and remains in terrible pain. The wounds never mended properly. No matter what the doctors have done to try to heal him, he awakens each morning in agony."

"That's how he ended up next door," Tynan said, his voice barely above a murmur. "Each night he goes to that opium den to relieve the tormenting pain."

She released a breath and nodded. "I want to take him home. I want to get him to the Whitpool estate by the seashore that he loves so much. I want to get him away from London and the bad influence of his friends. But I can't do it alone and no one will help me."

She gazed at him with her big, brandy-colored eyes.

Bollocks.

He only needed to give a responsive nod in sympathy. She wasn't asking for his help. She was merely relating her tale of woe.

"Abigail…" *Shut up, you idiot.*

"Yes, my lord?"

He groaned.

What tempest was he about to sail into?

CHAPTER TWO

"WE'LL HAVE TO form a plan," the Earl of Westcliff said, ignoring the fact that he didn't know Abigail and owed her no obligation whatsoever. Quite the opposite, he'd saved her life. She was the one indebted to him.

Abigail gaped at this exquisite man with smoldering eyes that were the color of emeralds. A rich, dark green, flecked with the soft gray of burnt embers. He was big and brawny, not to mention handsome as sin. He'd told her that she could call him Tynan. Or Ty. She would call him her miracle angel, if he'd let her. "Are you saying that you'll help me?"

He raked a hand through his head of wavy, blond hair. "Yes."

Her fingers tightened around the bedpost, but what she really wanted to do was hold onto him. She wanted to rest her head against his broad shoulders and cry in relief that someone… finally… someone was going to help her.

But what fool would jump into such a situation?

The Earl of Westcliff had none of the vapid inanity one would associate with idiocy. Indeed, he was the farthest thing from foolish she could imagine. His brooding, dark gaze was sharp and assessing. No, this was a clever man, but not one who gave the impression of being particularly charitable. What favor would he seek from her in return? Perhaps he wasn't her miracle angel after all. "I don't understand. Why would you help me?"

He raked a hand through the thick waves of his hair again. "In truth, the reason eludes me. It could be because I have brothers, too. In many ways, Peter reminds me of my own cousin, James. He's the Earl of Exmoor and I want you to meet him. I think it is important that you do."

She nodded, deciding not to think too hard about his motives. He had saved her life tonight in more ways than one. "I look forward to it. Why does your cousin remind you of Peter?"

"James was wounded quite badly during the war, physically and… I don't quite know how to explain his other injuries. They weren't the sort of wounds one could see. His soul was shattered. We weren't certain he would ever recover from that."

"I understand. Skin heals. Broken bones mend. But how does one restore a lost soul?" She pursed her lips in thought. "You speak as though his torment is a thing of the past. What happened?"

Westcliff smiled. "Love happened."

She leaned forward, eager to hear more. "Ah, love is the miracle cure for many ills. I believe that, I truly do." But was a sister's love for a brother enough to work a miracle on Peter? She understood that Westcliff was speaking of a different sort of love, the kind shared between a husband and wife. "Your cousin is very fortunate. I look forward to meeting his wife. She must be someone quite special."

The earl's nicely formed lips cracked wide as his smile broadened. "She is. You'll like Sophie. You remind me a little of her. Soft on the outside, but forged of steel on the inside."

Abigail shook her head and sighed. "You mistake me, my lord. I am soft and gooey inside and out. I haven't helped my brother. Sometimes, I worry that I may have been too spineless and allowed him to fall into this abyss he seeks out nightly. I should have been doing all in my power to save him. We Crofts are headstrong. I pleaded with him, but he wouldn't listen."

"His situation isn't your fault."

"I try to convince myself of it, but the "ifs" plague me. *If* he hadn't chosen to be a soldier. *If* he'd gotten better care. *If* I'd found him a better doctor. *If* I'd been there sooner to tend to him. *If* I'd fought harder to–"

"Stop, Abigail. Why do you impose this burden on yourself? You can't fix everything. You can't make people behave as you think they ought to behave. You can't make them perfect."

She nodded, knowing he was right and still feeling helpless about her brother's slow and painful decline. "I'm not very good at business matters either. I understand what tasks need to be accomplished in order to maintain the Whitpool properties, but I can't seem to carry them out on my own."

"Bollocks," Westcliff muttered, rising from his chair and moving to his mirror to fidget with the cravat he'd just grabbed out of his bureau and was now trying to form into a fashionable knot.

She studied him.

He was so handsome, he stole her breath away. He reminded her of a

Roman gladiator, big and muscular and agile. Her heart had shot into her throat when he'd first stepped onto the street with his pistols drawn and wearing nothing but his boots and trousers. He'd appeared strong and invincible then and still did now, although he was now fussing and fumbling with the folds of silk, unable to make a decent knot.

She found this surprisingly endearing.

Other than failing at a task that any valet could master within a few minutes, did he have a weakness? If he did, she couldn't find it. No, this gladiator was perfect. The fact that he was making an unfashionable mess of his cravat made him even more so. She smiled inwardly. True perfection was dull and dismaying. She liked that he couldn't fashion a proper knot. "Let me help you." Laughing, she rose from his bed to come to his side.

Good gracious!

From his bed?

She must have been more distressed than she realized, giving little thought to where she was… in his bedchamber… in his bed, and she was the one who'd foolishly asked for permission to sit there.

Yet, she now felt safe with this man.

It had not escaped her notice that he was putting *on* his clothes. Slowly, to be sure. First his shirt. Then his vest. Now his cravat. But it proved he was a gentleman at heart, one who would keep to his word.

He turned to her, wordlessly staring down at her as she put her trembling hands on the fine, green silk and began to fold and tuck the ends until they'd made a perfect knot at his throat. Up close, he was even bigger than he'd first appeared. His muscles, those that she'd grazed while working the sleek fabric into place, were granite-hard and taut.

She took a deep breath to compose herself, for this divine gladiator overwhelmed her. But it was a mistake to take that breath. His sandalwood scent surrounded her. *He* surrounded her, hot and male and rugged.

He made her weak in the knees.

Was there anything *not* wonderful about this man?

Of course, he was in a gentleman's club and must have been engaged in dissolute and utterly deplorable activities before she'd interrupted him. Said deplorable activities must have been abruptly cut off when he'd run downstairs to rescue her. The heavy scent of exotic perfume lingered in the air, causing Abigail's nostrils to twitch in irritation.

She sneezed. "Ugh, gardenias." The woman he'd been with must have bathed in it, the odor was so strong. She sneezed again. "I mean. It's none of my business who you bring up here." She held her breath, feeling another tingling itch in her nose. "*Achoo.* But, how can you stand it?"

The gladiator earl withdrew his handkerchief and handed it to her. "It is strong," he admitted with a grimace. "That's why I was standing by the window. I'd just opened it when I saw you on the street."

She turned away from him and crossed to the window, suddenly curious to know what he'd seen when peering out of it. She poked her head out and viewed the entire street. It was a clear, unobstructed view. That's why he'd seen those three blackguards approaching her. Thank goodness. She wouldn't have noticed them until they were almost upon her.

Another man might have ignored her peril, shut the window, and returned to his carnal pleasures.

But the Earl of Westcliff had run downstairs to save her.

She turned to face him, curious to know whether he'd sent the woman away.

If so, where was she now?

"She isn't coming back." His gaze was on her lips, and she realized that she was nibbling her lower lip, something she often did when puzzling out a problem.

She gasped, embarrassed that he could read her thoughts. "How did you know what I was thinking?"

"Those big, brandy-colored eyes of yours," he said, his voice warm and husky. "They hide nothing."

He took a step toward her so that he was standing too close.

Deliciously close.

He tipped his head toward hers and leaned forward. Was he going to kiss her?

More important, was she going to let him?

"Abigail, might I…" The deep, resonant timbre of his voice sent a thrill up her spine and through her limbs. "That is… would you…"

"Yes." It suddenly seemed vitally important that her first kiss should be with someone meaningful, not to mention devastatingly handsome and knowledgeable about such matters. The earl easily met all those requirements. He'd saved her life. He was handsome enough to make a girl swoon. He was rakish enough to make her first kiss unforgettable.

She was about to close her eyes and tip her head up, when he breathed a sigh of relief and moved away. "Thank you. I do not wish to impose on you. Or insult you in any way. But I can't put these blasted things on my cuffs without help and I can't very well summon my valet while you're in here." He held out his hand, palm up, to reveal two shiny, gold squares with a large W etched into each square.

Cufflinks?

Her stomach sank into her toes.

That's what he wanted? Not a kiss, but a valet to help him put on his cufflinks. "Yes. I'm happy to help. No insult taken, my lord. None at all. My, they're splendid. Are they heirlooms carried down through the generations from Westcliff earl to Westcliff earl?" She sighed. "We have no such traditions, unfortunately. The Whitpool barons seem to take turns finding new and destructive ways to tarnish the title." She was rambling now, too ashamed to admit her disappointment in not receiving a kiss, and too appalled to think she would have allowed it.

That was an understatement.

She was giddy for his touch, craved to feel the warmth of his lips pressed against hers.

Suddenly, it was the only thing that mattered. She'd been without warmth for so much of her life.

She hadn't missed it before, not like this.

Her brothers had loved her, but three of them were already gone. Now, Peter was slipping away. She couldn't bear it. There was a gaping hole in her heart, one that was growing wider by the day. A gaping hole and an aching need for someone to fill the painful void it had created, someone to hold her, to be strong for her, to assure her that everything would turn out sunshine and roses.

She took one of the cufflinks from the earl's outstretched palm. "I'll do your right wrist first, my lord."

"Tynan."

She nodded. "Quite so."

It was a tactical impossibility to put the little gold square through his cuff without touching him. His skin was warm. His hands were big. Hers were small and shaking. "Who would have thought it? My father sired four sons and not one of them managed to sire a son of their own, legitimate or otherwise, to carry on the title. Peter is the last hope. I suggested to him that it is his duty to carry on the family name, but he merely scoffed at me."

She switched to his left wrist and began to fuss with that gold link. "He doesn't want a wife. He doesn't want to secure the family's future. Sometimes, I think he doesn't want to live. Not like this." She took a deep breath. "He's in so much pain. I don't know how to help him."

Had she said too much?

Would he now retract his offer of assistance?

Why couldn't she just keep her mouth shut? "Forgive me, my lord."

"Tynan."

"Yes, indeed." She swallowed hard. "I don't usually chatter like this. In truth, I never chatter. Not that you'd ever guess because I'm still... chattering."

"Abigail," he cupped her cheek in the rough, warm palm of his hand. "I know I said I'd have my driver bring my carriage around to take you home, but would you mind waiting a little while longer? I can't leave for another hour yet." He frowned lightly. "I don't want you returning alone to an empty house. Let me escort you to your door."

She smiled in appreciation, trying not to be so obvious in her desperation to soak in every ounce of his kindness and his comforting touch. "I won't be alone. We keep a staff of six at our townhouse. They're very protective of me. They think I'm safely asleep in my bed."

His frown deepened. "How will you get back inside? Don't you lock your doors at night?"

"Oh, yes. We do." His hand was still on her cheek and she was still absorbing his ruggedly gentle touch. She cleared her throat. "Um, I climbed out of my bedchamber window. There's a trellis that hugs the wall directly under it. All I need to do is climb back up the trellis and haul myself over the sill. I left my window slightly open."

"You might fall." He slipped his hand from her cheek. "I'll bring you to the front door."

"Oh, no. You mustn't." She shook her head vehemently. "You'll only disturb my staff. Don't they have enough to worry about? But I'd be most grateful if you'd help me sneak back inside. The trellis was a little wobbly. You can hold it for me. I'd appreciate that, my lord."

"Tynan."

"As you wish."

He laughed softly. "Why won't you call me that?"

Heat soared into her cheeks, not to mention every other part of her body, for he had a dangerous effect on her. "I've known you less than half an hour. It feels improper."

He arched an eyebrow in obvious surprise. "Are you serious? You're in my bedchamber in a not-so-proper gentlemen's club, in the middle of the night, and you've already seen me half naked."

"But you're fully dressed now." Oh, my. She certainly had seen him unclothed and her heart was still dancing a merry tune because of that sight. A lively Highland jig, to be specific.

He turned away to retrieve his jacket, donning it while she gaped at him. It seemed a dreadful shame to cover up those spectacular muscles. It also struck her as odd that he was now fully clothed. Didn't such arrangements usually work the other way around? The parties in question walked in fully clothed and then stripped off their garments to engage in who knows what, because she certainly didn't know what that *who knows what* was that took place in the privacy of a bachelor earl's tawdry nest.

But she was eager to learn.

Would he teach her?

No! No! She couldn't let this man distract her. "My lord, you are to be commended for behaving honorably… for the most part. You should not have lifted me over your shoulder to carry me upstairs."

He appeared amused by her attempt to berate him. "Would you have come willingly?"

She sighed. "No, I suppose not. I'd just met you. I didn't know whether you were more dangerous than those drunken oafs."

He was standing close to her once more. She felt the soft whisper of his breath against her ear. "And now, Abigail? Would you come willingly if I asked you now?"

Oh, heavens! Yes. Was there a doubt? She licked her lips that suddenly felt parched. "Does it matter? I'm already here."

His smile turned wistful, perhaps mirthless. "So you are. The little rabbit in the wolf's lair." He drew away and rubbed his hand across the back of his sinewed neck. "Come on, little rabbit. Let's get you home before this wolf has a change of heart and eats you for dessert."

CHAPTER THREE

TYNAN HAD JUST walked downstairs to see if Coventry or Wainthorpe or any of the other earls in their circle had shown up this evening, when Wainthorpe walked through the front door. "Perfect timing," Tynan said, drawing him aside before he'd had the chance to remove his hat and gloves. "I need a favor. Some urgent business has come up and I must leave for a couple of hours."

Wainthorpe's gaze drifted to the top of the stairs. Abigail had come out of his room and was now spying on the two of them. Well, she was merely peeking at them out of curiosity. There was nothing clandestine going on, other than his wanting to get her home unnoticed by anyone at the club.

That plan was now shot to bits.

Wainthorpe gave a throaty chuckle. "Who's the partridge with the beautiful eyes? I gather she's your urgent business."

"She's no one you need to know about." *Bollocks, I'm not sharing Abby. She's mine.* "The blasted girl has a mind of her own. I told her to stay out of sight." He frowned at his companion. "Keep your hands off her. She's innocent."

"Am I to believe you had her all to yourself and did nothing about it? What's wrong with you? Having an off night?" Wainthorpe held up his hands in mock surrender when Tynan growled low in his throat.

"You may have your fun at my expense another time, Wainthorpe." Tynan needed him to take over his duties. "Will you watch the club while I'm gone?" Not that any of them had much to do other than remain close at hand in the event an unfortunate incident arose. This was a tightly run pleasure club. Guests were banned for life if they misbehaved.

Well, they all misbehaved.

The point was to be discreet about it and not cause a scene.

Wainthorpe gave a curt nod. "Yes, but watch yourself. It's the innocent ones who will cut you down at the knees." He didn't ask how Abigail got here or why. Tynan appreciated his companion's respect for privacy. He'd have to tell the Earl of Coventry about her though. He was their patron, their father figure, and would demand answers.

Tynan had no hesitation confiding in Coventry. Indeed, in telling any of his fellow earls, for he would need their help to keep Abigail's brother away from the dangerous pleasures offered next door. He already had the beginnings of a plan in mind, but was not ready to share it with Abigail or anyone else yet.

He knew the Wicked Earls could be counted on to do whatever he needed them to do when the time came. Although they kept their connections quiet, they all took their club membership and the responsibilities it implied quite seriously. The W emblem discreetly pinned to their lapels or on the stickpins adorning their cravats could just as well have been a B to stand for brotherhood.

He and Wainthorpe made a quick inspection of the gaming hell, the private card room where the higher stakes wagering took place, the dining room, and the hallways that led to the private chambers where games of quite another sort took place. "All appears under control," Wainthorpe said. "Go on, I've got it covered."

Tynan mumbled his thanks and hurried toward the stairs. A woman he recognized as a marchioness emerged from a nearby room. Her gaze turned predatory when she saw him striding down the hall. "I'm cold, Westcliff. Care to warm me up?" She thought to tempt him by allowing her robe to fall open, baring her breasts to him.

"Can't tonight, m'lady." Not that he would have done so on any other night. The marchioness enjoyed multiple companions and he wasn't the sort to share. Or take another man's leavings. No buttered bun games for him. He kept walking. *Bollocks.* Was Abigail still peeking on the stairs? He ran up them two at a time, his heart in his throat, although he didn't know why he should be so worried about her delicate sensibilities. She'd gotten herself into this fix, even if it was for noble reasons. He was no monk. The girl could not be so dense as to think he was.

He strode in and stopped dead in his tracks.

Abigail's slender body was bathed in a silvery beam of moonlight, her shoulder casually propped against the wall while she gazed out the window onto the street below. But it was what she held in her hand that caught his attention, and what she was doing with it that had his heart now pounding like thunder in his chest.

The blasted peacock feather.

She ran it slowly across her cheek. Her head tipped back slightly and her eyes fluttered closed as she slid it slowly... sensually, down her neck.

Sweet merciful heaven.

"Abby." He cleared his throat, wishing he hadn't promised to keep his hands off the girl. Stupid idea. His body was in torment. He wanted to put his hands all over her.

He closed his eyes a moment, hoping to expunge the wicked thoughts whirling in his head. Indeed, he wanted this girl with a hunger he'd rarely felt before. The ache to hold her in his arms, to explore the wonders of her body with his hands and lips... even with that blasted feather... was new to him, and he wasn't certain that he liked it.

Was she purposely doing this to him?

Bollocks, he knew she wasn't.

Which made his torment all the greater.

She turned to him, a vision illuminated by the moon's silver glow. "Lord Westcliff, I didn't hear you come back in."

"Tynan."

"Precisely." She cast him the softest smile. "I had no idea peacock feathers were so soft."

"Give me that." He strode to her side and took it out of her hand, practically tossing it across the desk. He ought to have tossed it out the window, but she'd probably find it and retrieve it, and then she'd be playing with it in his carriage during their ride to her home. She'd tortured him enough for one evening. "It isn't yours."

"I know. I wasn't hurting it." She frowned at him. "I wasn't going to steal it, if that's what has you worried. Why are you so protective of that feather, anyway?"

"I'm not." He took her by the elbow. "Let's go."

He peered out the door and down the hall to make certain no one else happened to be about. He did the same as they walked downstairs.

All clear.

By the giggles he heard coming from the room that the marchioness occupied, he realized she'd found a partner or two to indulge her in her games of pleasure.

He moved Abby along before she heard more than was appropriate for her innocent ears. As soon as they stepped out of the club, she tensed and gazed up and down the street. "Do you think those men might still be lurking about?" she asked.

"No, they're gone."

She nibbled her lip. "How can you be sure?"

He forced his gaze from her lips before he foolishly kissed her. "Our footmen chased them off."

"They did?" She breathed a sigh of relief. "Thank them for me, please."

He nodded and helped her climb into his carriage. His heart began to pound a hole through his chest the moment he circled his hands around her waist to help her up. He'd touched women before and far more intimately.

This girl felt different.

She felt like heaven.

She sank back against the plush leather squabs, watching quietly as he climbed in after her and took the seat across from hers.

"My lord–"

"Tynan."

"Indeed. Do you think we might venture next door and–"

"Not a chance." He knocked on the roof to signal his driver to take them to the Whitpool townhouse in Mayfair. The carriage jerked forward when the driver snapped the reins. Abby almost fell onto his lap, but she caught herself in time.

Too bad.

"You're not going anywhere near that den of iniquity. You're not ever to go near it or even think about going near it again." He frowned to emphasize his point, although it was too dark in the carriage for her to see his face beyond its shadowed contours. He could barely make out the soft curves of her body, or the angry rise and fall of her bosom as she inhaled the crisp, October air while debating whether or not to tell him just where he could shove his commands.

"Thank you, my lord. I'll take your suggestion under consideration." Her clipped tone revealed she wished to do quite the opposite of thanking him.

He wanted to laugh at the tactful way she'd just told him to go to hell, but this was no frivolous undertaking. She'd almost been assaulted tonight, he could not allow her to continue her foolish quest. "Abigail, that house is too dangerous even for me. It may have started out as an artist salon, but no art displays or poetry recitals take place there now. It is an opium den."

She sat quietly for a moment, then sighed. "You're right, of course. We'll deal with Peter when he comes home. I won't go there again."

They fell into a longer, companionable silence.

He did not need to see her or touch her to feel this girl's presence. Her nearness was enough to put his senses in a mad spin. Her occasional sigh was enough to send his iron control careening off a cliff.

He was eager for their ride to end. The subtle scent of roses on her skin had now mingled with the warming air in the enclosed carriage and was setting off ridiculous fantasies in his brain. He'd known the girl less than three hours… not even two hours.

How could she be having this effect on him?

She was not the usual sort of young woman he encountered. In truth, she was an unexpected breath of fresh air.

He could feel her hopeful innocence surround him.

Not too sweet. Not cloying.

Just intoxicating.

"Tynan," she said, her voice barely above a whisper as the carriage rolled down the street. She spoke so softly, he almost didn't hear her. "Thank you for everything. No matter what happens next, I'll never forget your kindness this evening or your offer to help me with my brother. I hope you won't wake up in the morning and realize you've just made a foolish mistake. I'll forgive you if you decide never to see me again. But I want you to know how grateful I am for your generous offer of assistance."

She'd called him Tynan. Finally. He didn't know why it mattered so much. "Abby, I gave you my word and I'll keep to it."

"I don't want you to. I mean… I want you to, but not if it is a burden to you. It feels so good just knowing that you offered and that I would not be struggling alone. I needed that support today. I'd reached the end of my rope and could not have managed another moment. You caught me as I was about to break into a thousand pieces. But I won't break now. I'm put back together for a while longer. A good long while. So… thank you."

The girl may as well have clamped his heart in a vise and twisted it. Repeatedly. If he'd ever considered abandoning her, the thought had now fled his mind. He was determined to help her. Saving her brother was now his sacred quest.

Bollocks.

He knew better than to believe he could do it.

He'd try though.

He wanted a happy ending for Abby, but didn't think it was possible. He would be there to console her when the worst happened. It wasn't a question of *if*. He knew her brother was too far gone.

"Tynan, is there anything I can do for you to repay this favor?"

She didn't know what she was asking. Yes, she could do something for him. Spend a night of pleasure in his arms. Give herself to him, body and soul. He'd never ask it of her, for he was afraid that one night would surely turn into a thousand nights. Then a thousand more. And another thousand more. Would he ever tire of this beautiful innocent?

"There is one thing you can do for me, Abby."

"Anything," she said, far too eagerly and casting him a disarming smile.

"Spend the day with me tomorrow. I'll come around to pick you up at noon. James and Sophie have invited me for lunch. I'd like you to meet them as soon as possible."

"Your cousin, the Earl of Exmoor, and his wife?" Her smile turned to one of genuine delight. "I'm eager to meet them, but won't it be rude of me to arrive at their doorstep unannounced?"

"I'll send word for them to add you. They won't mind. It will just be the four of us. It's important that you meet them. James will be able to help us get into Peter's thoughts. He'll understand what Peter is going through since he went through bad times himself. Sophie rescued James. I'm hoping she'll have some good advice for us as well."

He felt the soft touch of Abby's hand as she leaned forward and placed it over his. "I'll be ready." She kept it on his a moment longer before drawing it away. "Oh, my home is just around the corner. Have your driver stop here and I'll climb over the wall. I don't want my neighbors to see me."

Tynan rapped on the roof.

The driver tugged on the reins and drew the horses to a stop. "I'm coming with you. You said the trellis was loose. I'm not leaving until I know you've made it safely up to your bedchamber."

He grinned into the darkness when he heard her little huff. "Very well, but I can manage this part. I purposely wore my sturdiest boots and this practical gown."

"The gown isn't practical. It has too many buttons."

"Only down the front," she said. "I am adept at unfastening buttons."

He gave a throaty laugh as he opened the carriage door. "So am I."

It took her a moment to grasp the import of his words. "Well... I'll just keep that in mind." Despite the coolness of the night air, he could feel the heat of her blush. "I didn't realize you'd noticed my... buttons. You've had years of practice coaxing ladies out of their gowns, no doubt. But if... Tynan, please promise me you'll keep your hands off my... um, buttons."

He leaned forward and gently cupped her chin in the palm of his hand. "I'll do no such thing. I give you fair warning, Abby. I gave you my word as a gentleman tonight. But no man is ever a true gentleman. If I catch you traipsing about at night on your own again, all wagers are off. I will have my way with you next time."

"What exactly does that mean? *Have my way with you.*" She climbed out of the carriage and waited for him to follow. "It's a ridiculous expression."

"Its meaning is obvious. I shouldn't have to explain it." He helped her over the low wall that separated the Whitpool townhouse from the street, silently cursing the lightning bolt of heat that shot through him when he placed his hands on her waist. "Where is your bedroom?"

"Over here," she said in a whisper, taking his hand to guide him toward the trellis.

Now that his eyes had adjusted to the darkness, he could make out more than vague shapes under the moon's bright glow. But Abby didn't have to know it. He liked holding her hand. He wished to do more, but was not about to act upon his urges.

"Good night, Tynan." She gave his hand a light squeeze, then hiked her gown to her knees and began to climb up the trellis. She was graceful, for the most part, except when it came to heaving herself over the sill and into her room. He heard her grunt several times, and then he heard a thump as she toppled inside.

"Gracefully done, my little rabbit," he whispered with a chuckle. He shook his head, knowing he should not be enjoying this unusual girl's company as much as he was.

She stuck her head out, and he noticed that she was rubbing her brow. "I'm fine. Just a little bump."

"You landed on your head?"

"On my forehead," she insisted, as though it made a difference. "I'll see you tomorrow. Thank you again. Oooh, I feel like Juliet at her balcony, looking down upon her Romeo. Will you spout odes to me?"

"No, you little nuisance. Get inside. Go to bed." He made his way back to his carriage without giving her another glance.

"Bollocks, that girl is trouble." He thought of Abby as his little rabbit, but in truth, he was the one in danger of being snared by her beautiful, brandy eyes.

Bah! I'm a wolf. I eat rabbits.

So why did he feel that Abby had just taken a big bite out of him?

CHAPTER FOUR

ABIGAIL AWOKE TO the sun spilling onto her bed and warming her cheeks. She could tell by the height of the sun over the rooftops that she'd overslept. "Tynan," she muttered, tossing the covers aside and hopping out of bed. She wanted to look her best when he came around to pick her up.

"Did you say something to me, Miss Abigail?"

"Oh, Sally! I hadn't noticed you there. No, I was just mumbling to myself." Her maid was sitting quietly in a corner of her bedchamber, sewing the hem of the gown she'd worn last night.

"I don't know how the fabric came undone, Miss Abigail. I noticed it as I was preparing your wardrobe for today." The girl shook her head and sighed. "One would think you'd been climbing trees. There's bits of grass and leaves stuck to it, but I could have sworn it was clean when I stowed it away."

The chime of the tall clock in the hallway caught Abby's attention. She counted each chime and breathed a sigh of relief when the clock fell silent at the count of ten. She had two hours before Tynan called upon her. "Has my brother come home yet?"

Sally nodded. "Only about an hour ago. Oh, he looks wretched. Vickers offered to bring up some food for him, but he refused it and fell onto his bed without bothering to take off his boots or clothes. Not even his cloak."

She saw that Sally was getting overset, but this was the way it had been lately, the entire household upended by Peter's behavior. There was nothing any of them could do about it. Abby came to Sally's side and took her hand. "I'll look in on him once I'm washed and dressed. I have to look my best this morning."

Sally's ears perked. "Is something important going to happen today?"

She nodded. "I hope so. I met a gentleman... er, recently." She was about to let slip that she'd met Tynan last night, but caught herself in time.

Sally squealed. "A young man who's taken an interest in you? A beau?"

Abby laughed and shook her head. "No, nothing like that. He's going to help me save Peter. His cousin went through similar difficulty and he offered to help my brother pull through."

The girl did not appear convinced, but she smiled kindly at Abby. "Miss Abigail, we'll all pray as hard as we can for that miracle to happen." She paused a moment, clearly wishing to say more. "But... whether or not his lordship gets better... will you not think of yourself? If this gentleman is not a beau, then it's time for you to think about finding one."

"I'm only twenty. I doubt anyone would consider me stale goods yet."

Sally frowned at her. "The sister of a baron is in a far better position to find herself a husband than a young woman with no family to support her. I'll say no more. It isn't my place. But his lordship isn't the only one we worry about and pray for."

"I know and I appreciate it. Come, help me get ready. I think I'll wear the green wool with the ivory lace trim." Sally set out a matching shawl. Even though the sun was shining and the sky was a deep, rich blue, there was no mistaking the approach of winter.

While Sally prepared her bath, Abby tossed another log onto the small fire that was already blazing in the hearth, for there was still a slight chill to the room.

Perhaps it was merely the persistent chill in her bones, that feeling of impending doom. No, she wasn't going to give up or lose hope.

It didn't take Abby long to ready herself for the day. She went downstairs and sat alone in the dining room for half an hour, her hands warmed by the cup of hot cocoa she slowly drank. She knew the earl would arrive soon.

Or had she conjured this perfect man in her dreams? Did he really exist?

She set aside her cup and rose to check on Peter. His valet, Vickers, had spent the last hour trying to coax him into having a light repast, but to no avail. She would try now. Her brother had lost so much weight these past two months, he resembled a skeleton. The entire household was alarmed. His doctors had done all they could to help him. Finally, they'd told her to get him out of London before it was too late.

She wanted to do just that, but Peter was still baron and had countermanded all her orders. He'd had enough presence of mind to cut off her allowance so that she'd have no funds at her disposal to rent a carriage or open the baronial manor house or pay for Bow Street runners to forcibly drag him there.

"Peter, are you awake?" She rapped lightly at his door. "Peter, I'm coming in."

She didn't care if he tossed objects at her head, he wasn't going to chase her out. In truth, he was probably in too deep a slumber to hear anything even if she blew a trumpet in his ear. The room was dark, the yards of heavy silk drapery tightly drawn so that not a single ray of light shone in. One of the footmen had lit a small fire in the hearth when Peter first arrived, but it was already dying out, the last of its golden glow about to fade.

Just like Peter.

"I'm going out for the afternoon, Peter. Please have something to eat before I go. I'm so worried about you."

The silence was deafening.

But he was still alive, for she heard his raspy breaths. If the opium did not kill him, the night chill would. He was so weak and frail now. She sat on the bed beside him and touched his cheek. "The bread is freshly baked and warm. I could put a little marmalade on it for you. Would you like that?"

He refused to answer.

She stayed where she was, uncertain what to do next, so she caressed his cheek again and struggled not to burst into tears. But she wanted to cry big, aching tears of desperation and sorrow.

She took a deep breath and brought herself under control. Tynan should not see her like this now that he was bringing her a glimmer of hope.

"I love you, Peter." The tears rolled down her cheeks even though she'd tried to keep them away.

Then her composure completely shattered when her brother did the unexpected. "Love you, Abby." Just those three words, spoken into his pillow so that they came out muffled and raspy and almost unintelligible, but she'd heard them. Then he'd resumed snoring, his breaths just as strained, the wheezing just as pronounced.

Abby was not her cheerful, put-together self by the time Tynan arrived and was shown into the drawing room. She had spent the last ten minutes trying to stop the flood of her tears, but they simply wouldn't stop spilling down her cheeks. She was like a burst dike that sprang leaks everywhere and wouldn't stop overflowing.

Tynan took one look at her and shut the doors behind him. "Abby, what's happened?"

He strode to her side and drew her up against him, folding his big arms around her as he embraced her. "Tell me what's happened. Has your brother returned home?"

She nodded against his chest. "He's home."

"Then he's safe for now. Let me take you to James and Sophie's. We'll come up with a plan." He rubbed his hands up and down her back, rubbing warmth into her cold and shivering body.

"How can I go looking like this? I can't stop crying, and even if I did, my face will be red and blotchy." She wiped at her cheek with the soaked handkerchief in her hand. "What if I cry in front of them?"

"They'll understand." He took the tear-dampened handkerchief out of her grasp, replaced it with his own clean, dry one, and then waited for her to blot her tears and gather a little of her composure. "Feeling any better?"

She nodded, appreciating his patience and eager to confide in him. "Peter said he loved me. The old Peter is still there inside of him, the Peter who wants to live and be my brother again. The one who wants to laugh and be happy. I felt the ache of his heart straight through to my bones. Those words were his cry for help. But he's so weak, he can't fight for himself any longer."

She took a deep breath, at a loss to understand why this handsome earl with a thousand women eager for his attention would waste a moment of his time on her. "I thought he was fast asleep when I looked in on him this morning. He'd just returned home and immediately collapsed on top of his bed. That's his routine now. Sleep all day and destroy himself all night. My routine is to check on him every morning and tell him that I love him. He never answers me. But today he did. *Love you, Abby.* That's when I broke down." She swallowed hard, refusing to cry again. "I have to save him. I can't let him slip away."

"I know." Tynan trailed a finger lightly across her brow. "No bruising. Good." He held her a moment longer, and she had the feeling he'd hold her like this for hours if she wished it.

She did wish it, but they had work to do. "Shall we go? If you're still willing to take me with you, then I don't want to be late for your cousin's luncheon."

He cast her a tender grin. "Yes, but you'll walk out the front door this time. No leaping from bedroom windows."

She shook her head and laughed. "No more leaps, I promise."

Sally and Vickers were both standing in the entry hall as she walked out of the drawing room with Tynan. Oh, dear. The doors had been closed for privacy. Completely inappropriate, of course. But this was the least of her worries.

Vickers held out her cloak and Tynan helped her to put it on.

Sally held out a moistened handkerchief and instructed her to keep it over her eyes during the carriage ride. "He's the Earl of Westcliff," she whispered with a squeal, drawing her aside and pretending to fuss with her cloak. Sally's gaze remained embarrassingly fixed on Tynan. "Wherever did you find him?"

"Oh, I picked him up on the street last night." Which she had done, but no one needed to know the details.

Sally frowned. "Make a jest of it, if you will. But every debutante in London is after that gorgeous man. Yet, he wants you. Do not let him go."

Let him go? She was amazed that Tynan was not already running away as fast as his powerful legs would carry him.

Tynan escorted her down the front steps to his waiting carriage. She hadn't noticed its splendor last night, but there was no overlooking the magnificence of the gleaming, black conveyance with the impressive Westcliff crest embossed on the door. She sank onto the soft, leather seat she'd taken the night before. He settled across from her, seeming to dominate the interior with his naturally commanding presence.

The curtains were drawn back from the windows allowing sunlight to filter in. Now that she'd dried her tears, she also noticed Tynan clearly for the first time this morning. Sally wasn't exaggerating. He was easily the handsomest man in London, and a bachelor, it turned out. Abby hadn't thought to ask him about his marital status last night or even this morning. She hadn't considered that anything romantic would ever come of their acquaintance. No gentleman in his right mind would offer marriage to a girl with an addicted, sickly brother and no suitable fortune of her own.

Oh, but he did look wonderful dressed in shades of brown today, other than his shirt which was obviously a crisp white and impeccably Savile Row tailored. He wore buff-colored trousers and a dark brown coat, a silk vest in a patterned weave of browns and greens that picked up the color of his eyes, and a brown silk cravat that was perfectly knotted.

He grinned at her when he noticed the direction of her gaze. "My valet tied the knot. What do you think?"

She laughed softly. "I think you are fortunate to have him, and not me, as your valet. He knows what he is doing. I did not."

He cast her a devastatingly tender smile that reached into the dangerously, dark green depths of his eyes and made them gleam. "But your hands are softer. And I've never had the urge to take Melrose into my arms and kiss him senseless. He smells of furniture polish." He leaned forward and took the wet handkerchief from her hands. "Here, let me put it over your eyes as your maid directed. You'll feel better by the time we reach my cousin's house."

He spread the cool cloth over her eyes, the mere graze of his fingers against her skin shooting wild tingles through her. "Do I smell like furniture polish?"

He took a deep breath that tickled her neck and shot more tingle through her. "No." His voice was husky and wrapped around her like a caress. "Your scent is summer roses."

"What's yours? What have you got on today? You wore sandalwood last night." She took a turn inhaling him. *Oh, heavens.* Her heart exploded with excitement. How was it possible for any man to have such an effect on her? "Cinnamon today... and soap lather." He'd shaved.

She brazenly put a hand to his cheek, needing to feel the texture of his skin against hers. "Odd, you feel rough and smooth at the same time. Your jaw just tensed."

"You're touching me."

She drew her hand away, feeling slightly foolish that she'd been so easily carried away by the cinnamon and soap lather scent of him, and the clean, rugged heat of him. But she couldn't admit that to him. "With this cloth over my eyes, I couldn't see you. So I had to touch you... not that I had to... my eyes are feeling better. May I take the compress off now?"

"No, keep it on a while longer. You were crying very hard."

She nodded. "I couldn't help myself. Peter's words slipped through my defenses."

She heard him settle back in his seat, his broad shoulders easing against the firm leather padding. "I'm glad he wants to be saved, Abby. But he'll still fight like hell to defy you."

The resonant depth of his voice was doing odd things to her body. She was tingling, of course. Now her stomach was fluttering and her skin was flush with heat. She took the handkerchief off her eyes and gazed at him. "I'll fight harder. I want him back."

He smiled at her, but spoke no more as his carriage rolled up in front of a lovely house in Belgravia, not far from Hyde Park. Tynan hopped out and then turned to help her down. "I forgot to mention that my cousin has scars. I've grown so used to them, that I don't see them at all now. But you've never met James. The scarring is prominent on his face."

"I won't gawk."

He raked a hand through his hair. "I know, it's just that... I'm protective of him, as you are of your brother. I don't want you to think lesser of him because of his scars."

"Tynan, my brother is a skeletal shadow of himself. He's slowly killing himself by the day. He has sores on his body and hideous bruises. I think I can manage not to faint when I'm introduced to your cousin. If he's half as wonderful as you, I shall adore him." She inhaled lightly and groaned. "I mean... yes, that's exactly what I mean. You must be aware of my admiration for you."

"I wasn't. I wish you had told me earlier. I would have done something utterly rakish and improper about it." He smirked now, but his expression remained tender.

She inhaled lightly. "What would you have done?"

"Kissed you, for starters."

He'd caught her off guard with that comment. Her face suffused with heat. "What?"

"You heard me." He tucked her hand in the crook of his arm and led her up the couple of steps to the front door that was already open. "And if you don't stop looking at me that way, I'm going to kiss you right here and now."

TYNAN ENJOYED THEIR quiet meal more than he had enjoyed anything in years. The glazed duck and fish in *bechamel* sauce, although delicious, had nothing to do with it. Abby's smiles and gentle laughter, and her immediate acceptance of James was the reason.

He'd been so worried about her reaction to his cousin's scars, but he should have put his faith in her. Abby didn't ignore the scars. She merely accepted them, looked beyond them. Her easy manner was infectious and put them all at ease. "The fish is excellent, Sophie," she remarked, setting down her fork. "My compliments to your cook."

"Thank you, Abby. I shall let her know. She'll be pleased."

Tynan's chair groaned under his weight as he leaned back and stretched his arm across the empty seat beside him. The women were so friendly, one would think they were long lost sisters reunited for the first time in years.

The four of them were dining in the more casual winter dining room, but even this intimate, small table was large enough to comfortably accommodate ten. They were all at one end of it, Abby seated across from him and cozily ensconced between Sophie and James. As head of the household, James was at the head of the table and Abby was to his right, traditionally a seat of honor. Sophie was to the right of her. Tynan was seated to the left of James, all by himself on his side of the table.

Ridiculously, he missed being close enough to Abby to touch her, to inhale her delicate scent. He satisfied himself with watching her, something he could easily do while seated directly across from her.

Abby was similar in many ways to James' wife, Sophie. Beautiful, loving, and strong.

Sophie recognized the similarity as well.

She and James kept grinning at each other.

When they weren't grinning at each other, they were grinning at him.

One would think he'd brought the queen to dine here instead of the Honorable Miss Abigail Croft. In truth, it was a little insulting to see how relieved they were to see him with a respectable, young woman. Did they think he was a depraved Gorgon who ate young virgins for his supper?

He knew what they were thinking. Marriage. Now that James and Sophie were rollicking in wedded bliss, they wanted everyone to be happily married.

That included him.

Bollocks.

They'd better not tell his mother or his brothers about Abby.

He'd never hear the end of it.

More important, it wasn't fair to Abby. He didn't want anyone giving her the impression that he was serious about her. How could he be when he'd known her for less than a day? She was an acquaintance who needed his assistance. She was a diversion.

No, that wasn't quite right. To think of her as merely an amusement demeaned her unfairly.

She was a refreshing change from the debutantes who had nothing in their empty heads but the desire to marry the Earl of Westcliff. They wanted the title, wealth, and stature that came with such a union. He, Tynan Brayden, was irrelevant to these girls.

But he was important to Abby.

He liked that.

They got down to serious conversation as soon as the footmen had cleared away their plates. Abby spoke first, quietly telling them all about Peter.

More than ever, Tynan wanted to reach across the table to take her hands in his. She had them tightly clasped in front of her, probably to keep them from trembling. She spoke with a sober earnestness, but there was a quiver to her voice every once in a while, and he knew that this discussion was difficult for her.

He was relieved when James took over, and they all listened intently as he told Abby about his state of mind and the struggles he had endured upon returning to London. "I returned to a city I no longer recognized. It wasn't so much that London had changed, but I had changed. I did not view it with the same eyes. The parties I attended before the war no longer seemed splendid but shallow. The people I'd once dismissed out of hand now seemed so much more vital and interesting to me than those within my social circle." He sighed and shook his head. "And yet, I still wanted to belong in that social circle. That's what I had been raised to do. It's what I knew. But it had also become something I detested."

"Everything James did and felt was influenced by the constant pain in his leg," Tynan explained.

"That pain controlled him," Sophie said, her eyes turning watery. "It could have led him down any path."

"In truth, I was on the path to ruin when Sophie came into my life." James cast his wife a smile filled with affection. His smile faded a moment later as he continued. "I still have pain, but I also have hope now. That's what Sophie has given me. Hope and love. But sometimes, even that is not enough. I have a strong will, not everyone does. Peter's doctors are right to want him to leave London. Take him far away from temptation, Abby. Take him to the sea, let him watch the ebb and flow of the tides, and feel the salty wind on his face and the wet sand between his toes. Let him sail out in a boat, mend fishing nets, clean the barnacles off a boat's hull. Give him tasks to keep him occupied. His mind is frantic and needs to be distracted, not necessarily calmed."

Abby nodded. "I think I understand what you mean. He'd managed his pain while he was on the battlefield, for he had others to worry about and knew that their lives depended on his keeping his wits about him. He thinks that no one needs him now. As baron, he has only to ring for a servant, or sit with his estate manager, or summon his solicitors, and all will be done for him. I shall do as you suggest. I'll take him to the sea. We have a house on the southern coast–"

"No, don't take him there," Tynan said. "He's in charge there. Everyone will obey him, not you."

She paused a moment and cleared her throat. Tynan watched the pulse at the base of her neck begin to throb. "It isn't a perfect choice, I'll grant you. But I can't take him anywhere else. My brother controls my funds. As it is, I shall have to sell my jewelry to raise sufficient–"

Tynan emitted a soft growl. "Don't even think of it. I'll take care of the expenses."

Everyone suddenly gaped at him.

To his surprise, Abby's open-mouthed stare turned into a scowl. "You will not. I do not want your charity. Nor yours either, Lord Exmoor. I came here for guidance, not a hand-out."

Tynan slapped his hands on the table, further surprising them all... even himself. "Then I'll loan you the funds." This was no conversation to be having with the girl, even if he did trust James and Sophie to be discreet.

Abby was not at all pleased. "At what rate of interest? Even assuming I'll accept to borrow anything from you."

"You have no choice but to accept my help. You can't possibly raise enough funds to pay for a coach and driver, inns along the way, and stock a house with food and servants. Even if you did, what's to keep your brother from running back here at the first opportunity? You'll need someone with more authority than a baron to stop him."

He was now on his feet and angry with this girl for rebuffing his offer of assistance. In truth, he was angrier with himself for not merely wanting to help her, but *needing* to help her with every sweat and tear and ounce of blood in him. He hadn't known her a full day yet. Despite that obvious fact, he still felt as though he'd known her for all of his life. He knew her almost as well as he knew himself, possibly better, because he didn't recognize himself right now. "You'll need a staff who answers to that man of higher rank, who'll lock your brother in his room if necessary, and drag him back to sanctuary if he tries to run away."

You need me.

How loudly did he need to proclaim it?

Everyone was still gaping at him as though he'd gone mad and was howling at the moon. "Abby?" He gentled his tone because his own cousin was glowering at him and appeared ready to punch him in the nose. "Will you please accept my loan?"

She cleared her throat as she rose from her chair, and then calmly placed her hands on the table to mimic his stance. "Thank you, my lord. I shall take your offer under consideration."

He wanted to smile and at the same time throttle her. She had such a dignified way of putting him off. "Consider it and accept."

She cleared her throat again and nodded... well, it looked like a nod.

Was that a yes?

He met her gaze with a steady one of his own, determined to take nothing less.

CHAPTER FIVE

"ABBY, THERE IS no other way," Tynan said quietly, unrelenting in his determination to provide her the means to save her brother. They were now back in his carriage on their return ride to her home.

Abby knew she ought to have leaped at Tynan's offer, but something held her back. That something was her growing affection for him. She was like a moth to his bright flame and knew she would be burned by him if she got too close. "I liked your cousin and Sophie very much. Thank you for introducing them to me. I think Sophie and I will become good friends."

Tynan shifted his large frame to lean closer. "Why won't you accept my loan? You know it makes sense. I'm not asking for anything in exchange."

She nodded. "I know, but that's part of the problem. Your wonderfulness is overwhelming."

He laughed and groaned at the same time. "My wonderfulness? Abby, I'm a wretched hound."

"To others, perhaps. But you've been an answer to my prayers. You're an angel who swooped down from the heavens and rescued me. You are magnificent and generous and intelligent. The only thing wrong with you is that you don't know how to tie a proper knot in your cravat, but that doesn't really count since you have competent servants to do that for you."

"Wonderful and magnificent?" He arched an eyebrow, seeming to be genuinely surprised. Didn't all the women he seduced feel the same way? Was he not constantly being told this?

"You are so much more, Tynan. I've never met anyone as exceptional as you, and doubt I ever will. Of course, I want to accept your offer. I'd do anything to save my brother." She debated whether to say more and decided to simply tell him everything she was feeling because he'd probably guess it soon enough. "But if word got out that you had done this for me, I'd be ruined. Everyone would believe that... you know... they'd believe I had given myself to you."

"You're worried about that now? How is my loan different from your running off on your own at night? Or ending up in my private chamber at my club?" He folded his arms across his broad chest and awaited her answer.

"I'm a mere footnote. My actions are not newsworthy. Nobody knows me and nobody cares about me. But if I'm suddenly associated with you, London's most eligible bachelor, my every action will be splashed across the front pages of every gossip rag." She shook her head and sighed. "Even I read those scandal sheets. Everyone reads them. I am alone, as you well know. I own nothing but my good name. I'd like to hold onto it even if I lose everything else."

He unfolded his arms and ran a hand roughly through his hair. She was coming to recognize this habit of his whenever he was dismayed. "I hadn't thought of that," he admitted.

"Just give me time, Tynan. I will say yes. My brother is more important to me than the respect of Upper Crust strangers who don't care about me or my plight. But it isn't something I can blithely surrender in one afternoon." In truth, the worst part about losing her reputation was to lose it without the pleasure of truly being ruined.

He took a moment to digest her words, but his expression remained just as dogged and determined. "I know how to be discreet, Abby. No one will find out."

She rolled her eyes. "Everyone will know within a matter of days."

"Not if the funds appear to come from a respectable third party."

She inched forward in her seat. "What do you mean? That the funds would appear to come from your cousin? It is one thing to seek his guidance, but to involve him and Sophie too deeply in this plan is not a good idea. What if things go wrong? I don't want to create a problem between the two of you."

"I had someone else in mind, actually. Someone who will meet all your requirements. Not family. Very respectable. No hint of scandal will attach to him or you."

"Who is he?" They had almost reached her home and she was running out of time to ask questions. Even if she invited him in, Tynan would refuse. He had his own affairs to attend to. She'd already taken up his entire afternoon.

"I'd rather not tell you just yet," he said. "I'll speak to him tonight and let you know the outcome of our discussion tomorrow."

She nibbled her lip in worry. One more night lost in saving Peter. What if this man Tynan believed was the perfect solution said no? She'd simply have to trust Tynan's powers of persuasion, for he was persuasive indeed when he wanted to be. "Until tomorrow then. I usually wake up early. Call on me any time. Or sooner. I'll be home tonight taking care of the Whitpool business affairs that Peter has neglected. My door is always open to you."

He reached out and tweaked her chin. "Your open door? This evening? Now that's a tempting invitation. A little too tempting for me to handle. I'll let you know the gentleman's response tomorrow."

His carriage drew up to her front door. "I'll walk you in."

She allowed him to help her down, eager for the opportunity to touch him or be touched by him, no matter how casually it was done. In truth, her heart was not in the least casual about Tynan. She'd meant it when she'd told him that he was the answer to her prayers.

"I think your brother would enjoy Falmouth," he said, placing her hand in the crook of his arm as he walked her to the door. "It will suit all your requirements nicely. I think you will enjoy it as well."

"Falmouth? That's where your friend's property is located? I hear it's lovely there. Thank you, Tynan." That he'd been thinking of her situation throughout their carriage ride, even while peeved that she hadn't immediately agreed to his offer, touched her heart. "I'll write a note to James and Sophie to thank them for the lovely luncheon. Despite the difficult topics of conversation, it was the nicest afternoon I've had in ages. I wish you a pleasant evening. I'll see you tomorrow."

The door opened and she expected to find the Whitpool head butler, Jameson, standing beside it, but it was her own maid who'd flung open the door. "Sally, what's wrong?"

Tears were streaming down her cheeks. "It's his lordship. He's running a raging fever."

"Since when?" She hurried inside and hastily tossed off her hat and cloak. "It can't have been too long. He was fine when I left him a few hours ago."

Tynan followed her in and began issuing instructions to Sally. "Have the footmen bring up a tub and fill it with cold water. Ice, too. As much as you have available. Send one of the footmen to Dr. George Farthingale's office. Tell him the Earl of Westcliff wishes him to come at once."

He turned to Abby. "Where is your brother's bedchamber?"

"Top of the stairs. Follow me." She made no comment about the propriety of having him, a stranger, come upstairs. Peter's life was in chaos, and because of it, so was hers. She'd somehow gained the assistance of this rakish guardian angel, and knew her neighbors had just seen him follow her indoors. Rumors would begin to circulate within a matter of hours.

The only good to come out of this situation was that Peter might be too ill to visit his opium den for the next few days. "This is his door," she said, not bothering to knock before she barged in. The odor of vomit struck them as they walked into his room, an overpowering odor that permeated the air and struck Abby with the full force of a tidal wave.

Tynan strode across the room to draw aside the drapes and open the windows. "Abby, come here. Are you all right? You're turning green."

She wasn't all right. She was gagging and suddenly feeling weak in the knees.

He came back to her side and wrapped an arm around her shoulders, quickly guiding her to the open window. She poked her head out and gasped for fresh air. "I think I can manage now."

"Are you sure? Take your time. Breathe deeply, Abby. I've got you… for as long as you need."

She nodded. "It reeks in here. The odor caught me by surprise, that's all. I felt as though I was about to toss up my own meal. I'm better now."

"Do you want to wait downstairs for the doctor?" His manner was one of gentle concern and she wanted to thank him again for saving her as he'd done last night. She wanted not only to thank him, but to hold onto him with all her might because he was her gladiator angel and she didn't want to lose him. "Your footmen and I can discard his clothes and put him in the tub."

"No, I'll stay and help. He'll need fresh clothes. Vickers will put those out for him. I'll have one of the maids change his sheets." Within the hour, Peter was once more back in bed, this time a clean bed with clean sheets, and clean nightclothes. The ice water had done the trick to lower his fever and reduce the risk that he would once again fall into convulsions.

Abby had ordered the family cook to prepare a light broth in the hope that Peter might be able to hold some of it down in his stomach. She'd just gone downstairs to see about the broth when Dr. Farthingale entered. "Thank you for arriving so promptly," she said, letting out the breath of relief she'd been holding in all this time. The doctor was just as Tynan had described him, from his serious but gentle demeanor to the intelligence behind his deep blue eyes. "Lord Westcliff speaks so highly of you. He's upstairs now with my brother. Let me show you the way."

Abby escorted him into her brother's elegant baronial bedchamber, and wanted to protest when the doctor asked if she would mind leaving for a few minutes while he examined her brother. But Tynan took her arm in his and was already nudging her out of the room. "I'll walk downstairs with you, Abby. Dr. Farthingale will summon us if he needs us. Give him time to speak to Peter alone."

Of course, Peter would never open up to this man if she were hovering. "I'll ring for Jameson to bring us refreshments in the drawing room. In truth, I feel as though I need something stronger than tea." She gave a short, mirthless laugh, uncertain what would happen next. Peter was near death, his body too weak to fight the fever or convulsions now gripping him.

Tynan kept her arm in his while they made their way downstairs, and appeared reluctant to let her go once they entered the drawing room. "Sit down, Abby. I'll ring for your butler."

She sank onto the sofa, glad that Tynan was still here. She watched as he crossed to the bellpull to summon Jameson. After tugging the cord, he paused by the decanter of port sitting on a corner table. There were four crystal glasses beside the decanter. He took one and poured a little of the port into a glass. Wordlessly, he held it up to offer it to her.

She nodded. "I've never had it before."

"I think you can handle half a glass," he said with a small smile, handing her the glass and then returning to the side table to pour one for himself. "You've handled far more difficult matters on your own."

She twirled the glass slowly between her fingers. "Do you think Peter will confide in Dr. Farthingale?"

"I hope so. If anyone can get him to talk, it's Dr. Farthingale. He's seen it all, served in the military treating the wounded. I'll wager that your brother isn't the first injured soldier in dire straits that he's encountered." He took a swig of the port and moved to stand beside the fireplace, gazing into the flames for a moment before returning his attention to her.

He pursed his lips in thought as he studied her. She knew he was worried about her, or considering what to do with her, for she'd no doubt become a terrible nuisance to him. But he wasn't protesting or desperately striving for an excuse to leave and never come back. There was a quiet nobility about him, despite his wicked reputation, and she knew that he was going to remain by her side while the doctor was upstairs tending to her brother.

She took a sip of her port, coughed lightly and then grimaced before setting it down on the table beside her. "You don't have to stay with me if you don't want to. Indeed, how can you stand to be around me?" She clasped her hands together and gave another mirthless laugh. "At this time yesterday, we hadn't met. You were blissfully unaware of my existence and the havoc that was to come."

"I'm not sorry I met you, if that's what concerns you. It obviously does since you keep mentioning it and your every look is tentative, as though waiting for the moment I'll throw my hands up in frustration and simply walk away."

She said nothing in response, for he'd stated her thoughts precisely.

"Nor are you my pet project or charity case." He pursed his lips again as he gave his next words some thought. "You're a meaningful purpose, that's what you are. I've been given everything, an earldom, a loving family, decent looks," he said with the arch of an eyebrow.

She rolled her eyes. "Divine looks, you mean. There's no denying you're handsome."

"As I said, I've been given everything at little cost to myself. So do I just go forth and enjoy my bounty without a care for others? Or have I been given my advantages in order to do something worthwhile that no one else can do?" He crossed the room and settled beside her, his nearness causing her body to flood with warmth. "Abby, you mentioned earlier that your brother's situation worsened as his life became easier. Although his situation is far more perilous than mine, it is not much different from how I feel."

She met his contemplative gaze and listened intently as he continued. "My wicked reputation is earned, I won't deny it. But these frowned upon pursuits I engaged in were for the purpose of finding something to fill a void that has long existed inside of me. I enjoyed my carefree bachelor ways, but they were mere amusements. I didn't know how to fill this void until you came along."

What surprised Abby most was that he spoke of his bachelor activities as though they were a thing of the past. Was he done with the club and the idle pleasures it offered? Should she point out this slip of words to him?

She gave a little grunt, for it was not possible that she was responsible for adding purpose to his life. "Are you suggesting I've done you the favor and not the other way around?"

He shrugged his big shoulders and then casually rested his arm across the back of the sofa. When he stretched his long legs in front of him, she realized that he was making himself comfortable. He was showing no inclination to leave.

He took another swallow of his port, the deep red liquid sliding down his throat with an easy familiarity. It had tasted sweet, but too strong for her when she'd taken a sip, and now she felt a little lightheaded. Having never tasted anything stronger than ratafia before, she had yet to develop a tolerance for this simple dessert wine. The mix of spirits and stressful days had left her raw and vulnerable. All her worries were piling up and taking a toll on her.

"I would call our meeting one of mutual benefit," he said, drawing her attention back to him. "You needed help and I needed someone to need me. Well, damn... that sounds rather pathetic, doesn't it? I'm fine with my life. I'm not some wretch who is seeking constant attention or approval."

He rose abruptly and raked his fingers through his hair. "The thing of it is, had you truly been needy and grasping, I would have found a reason to back away. But you're brave, and I admire that in you. You're resolute in your purpose and are willing to sacrifice so much to save your brother, even at the cost of your own peril. You appreciate my assistance, yet you don't demand it of me. There's a strength in you. That's what draws me to you. Er, to your situation."

He drained his drink and crossed the room to pour himself another.

Abby took another sip of her own port. Where was Jameson with the tea cart? That Tynan admired her only increased the heat flowing within her body. By his own admission, he was a hound and that improper part of him would eventually come around to asking for something more from her, perhaps even her innocence, which was the only thing that was truly hers to give.

The sad part about it was that she hoped he would ask.

She set aside her glass and scowled at the ruby liquid that was putting reckless thoughts into her head.

Tynan knelt beside her. "Your cheeks are a bright pink. Are you all right?"

She put a hand to her cheeks. "Yes, I'm fine."

His smile was tender. "Your nose is a bright pink, too."

She gasped and her hand shot to it, but he took her hand in his to nudge it off her nose. "You're sensitive to port," he said with a chuckle.

"Oh, dear. I must look a mess."

"No, you look adorable. Like a little pink rabbit."

Her eyes grew wide as teacups. He was kneeling so close and she'd never expected him to be playful with her. "Are you going to kiss me?" Although why would he? She had a brother upstairs who had been vomiting and convulsing a mere hour ago, her face was a blotchy mess because she couldn't handle spirits in her system, and she was now hiccupping. Did handsome as sin earls kiss blotchy, rabbit-looking young ladies with hiccups?

His emerald eyes darkened and he cast her a smoldering glance. "Do you want me to?"

Yes.

"Only if you would care to." Her heart shot into her throat. That wasn't what she'd meant to say. She ought to have given him a firm rebuke, but he was her savior and she did not wish to deny him anything. Besides, what harm could there be in one kiss?

CHAPTER SIX

TYNAN OUGHT TO have known better than to encourage a conversation that could only end in a kiss between them. But Abby wasn't the only one hungry for it to happen. Perhaps it was for the best to simply lock lips with her and get it over with. Then they'd both be satisfied, their hunger and curiosity appeased.

He drew her to her feet along with him and wrapped one arm around her waist to draw her closer, but not close enough for their bodies to touch against each other. That would be too dangerous for both of them. He tucked a finger under her chin and tilted her head up at just the right angle to take his kiss.

Her beautiful brandy eyes were wide and she was hardly breathing. "Close your eyes, Abby."

He smiled in encouragement and watched her sooty eyelashes flutter shut and come to rest upon her delicate cheekbones. She'd taken a deep breath and had yet to let it out. His own breaths were coming faster now, as though this was his first time kissing a girl and the first time he'd inhaled the scent of summer roses against a girl's skin.

Bollocks.

What was happening to him?

He traced his thumb lightly across her fleshy, lower lip. *Soft.* So incredibly soft. He closed his eyes and lowered his lips to hers, eager to savor her with all of his senses. But he had no chance to savor, for every sensation welled up at once and struck him with the force of a tempest the moment his lips touched hers.

What he felt was a raging storm of desire, his heart now pounding like thunder while lightning bolts shot through his body, scorching a trail through every muscle and sinew with reckless and fiery abandon.

"Abby," he said in a whisper, wrapping his arms around her and drawing her up hard against him as he deepened what was meant to be a gentle, detached and proper kiss, but had become raw and hungry and possessive.

He growled low in his throat.

Wolf claims rabbit. Mine, Abby. You're mine.

Her body felt so good against his, her slender curves perfectly molding to his large frame, her pliant mouth surrendering to the demanding pressure of his. He loved the lush fullness of her lips, loved the eagerness of her response. This girl was a siren in disguise, her intoxicating call drawing him onto the rocks of destruction.

A kiss was not enough for him.

He felt wild and untamed, wanting to conquer her body, wanting to plunder her innocent core and embed himself fully inside of her.

He teased her lips apart, taking command and invading with his tongue, for he wasn't merely eager to probe and plunder the velvet warmth of her mouth. He was the hunter determined to corner his prey. He was the wolf on the prowl, and he meant to leave no doubt that she was his quarry, that she belonged to him, and he would never give her up.

She gave a breathy moan and gripped his shoulders.

He pulled her fully up against him, leaving not so much as a particle of air between them. His tongue slid along her lips and delved back into her mouth with desperate abandon. His hands possessively explored her body, roaming along her curves and igniting sensations of fiery desire within him, sensations that he'd never felt with any other woman before.

Hell, he'd gone too far with this girl.

But she didn't seem to mind. Quite the opposite, she arched against his body, seeming to crave his touch as hungrily as he craved hers. "Abby, push me away."

"No," she said with an ache to her voice that matched his own.

He crushed his lips against hers and held her so tight, their bodies molded into one. He knew he couldn't take this any farther. He couldn't seduce her into his bed. He couldn't remove the layers of clothes between them and touch her creamy skin, or taste her heat as he slid his tongue over the most intimate parts of her body.

He couldn't.

No matter how badly he wanted to.

"Abby? Are you all right?" His voice sounded raspy and breathless to his own ears as he ended the kiss and eased back gradually so that the storm of his desire and her own had time to calm.

"I am, Tynan. Thank you for asking." She opened her eyes and smiled up at him, her dark eyes sparkling and her smile broad and joyful. "I understand now why you're considered so devastating to women."

He frowned. "Did I hurt you?"

She shook her head in denial. "Not at all. I know you would never hurt me."

No, but he'd lost control in that moment, his lustful desires for this girl sweeping him along on its raging current. "I didn't mean to take it that far, not for your first kiss. I'm so sorry, Abby. I meant for it to be sweet and gentle."

"And I'd just lectured you on the importance of maintaining my good name." She laughed and shook her head. "I'm glad you weren't sweet or gentle. You gave me something unforgettable. You gave me a kiss to fill my dreams."

Bollocks.

She'd done the same for him.

Did he dare allow her into his heart?

"TYNAN, THAT KISS has changed things between us. Hasn't it?" Abby asked, concerned that he'd turned quiet and almost sullen since it happened.

She tried to act calm as she cut a slice of lemon cake for him and set it on his plate. "I know that you are a hound and this is what you do with women. Just because I loved it, doesn't mean that you owe me anything more or that I expect anything more of you."

His eyes widened and he glowered at her.

Perhaps she ought not to have used the word 'love' when speaking of the kiss. Obviously, using that particular word was like sticking a hot poker in him.

She handed him the plate of lemon cake, and then set it down with a clatter in front of him when he did not take it. "If you're going to be angry with me, then perhaps you ought to leave." She felt tears well in her eyes, but she refused to fall apart in front of him. "My only surviving brother is bent on destroying himself. He snarls and snaps and fights me at every turn. I don't need you doing the same. I *loved* your kiss." There, she was tossing the word in his face. "If you're bent on tarnishing my memory of it, then just go. I don't need another beautiful thing in my life ruined."

Tynan groaned. "Abby, I–"

She rose abruptly. "In truth, it's best that you leave. I'll wait for Dr.

Farthingale to finish examining my brother and come downstairs to talk to me. I don't need you here beside me."

Her voice caught and those last words came out sounding too much like a sob.

He got to his feet as well, now towering over her. Well, he was big. Gladiator big. "I have no intention of walking away from you."

"Oh, then I suppose you mean to run away." She motioned to the door. "Don't let me stop you."

He took her hand, this time growling to mark his annoyance with her. "If you must know, I'm behaving like a horse's arse because I enjoyed our kiss, too. Probably liked it more than you did. I'm not happy about this unexpected turn of events, that's all. I prefer to be in control. Always."

"Are you suggesting that I shattered your control?" Her eyes widened as she took in what he was saying. She had affected him. Merciful heavens! The possibility that *she'd* given *him* a kiss to remember for the rest of his days had never occurred to her.

"Shattered? That's a bit extreme. The point is, I'm angry with myself, not you." He cast her a sardonic smile. "So, may I stay? Because I have no intention of leaving your side until the doctor has given us his report, and I don't think you have the muscle to toss me out."

"I suppose you're right. It would cause an ugly scene." She laughed softly. "Poor Jameson's heart would go into spasm if he came upon us brawling." She turned serious now, but glad for the moment of levity. "I didn't mean what I said about not wanting you to stay. I'm so relieved that you're here to lend me support."

"I know, Abby."

"Then we are friends again?" She held out her hand to him.

He glanced at it. "Yes, we're friends. But I'm not going to take your hand. I'm not touching you again today."

She dropped her hand to her side. "For your sake or mine?"

He groaned. "Let's just say for both our sakes."

Abby nodded and had just resumed her seat on the sofa when Dr. Farthingale strode into the drawing room, a grim look on his face. She cast Tynan a desperate glance, wishing he hadn't just insisted on not touching her again. She felt cold and was afraid of what the doctor was about to tell her.

She clasped her hands together on her lap to keep them from trembling.

In the next moment, Tynan came to her side and took her hands in his, enveloping them in his warmth.

She cast him a surprised look. Hadn't he just resolved not to touch her?

"The hell with resolutions," he muttered. "You matter more."

Yes, she mattered to him today and perhaps tomorrow. Perhaps even for a few weeks. But Tynan would eventually figure out that she was not the one destined to fill whatever void he felt in his heart. Until then, she would enjoy his company and appreciate all his gestures of friendship and support.

She held her breath and listened as Dr. Farthingale spoke of her brother's situation, giving a cold, accurate assessment, and yet conveying obvious warmth and concern for his new patient. "Your brother came within a hair's breadth of dying today. His addiction has weakened his lungs and heart. He's too badly addicted to be taken off opium all at once. His heart will give out from the shock unless he's carefully eased off it," he warned.

Abby gasped. "What are you saying? That I'm to supply him with that lethal substance?"

He glanced at Tynan before returning his attention to her. "Someone has to do it. I'll do it if he remains in London. But I think it is too dangerous for him to be here among familiar surroundings. He knows where to go to feed his addiction and those vipers know how to reach him even if he doesn't come around to their den."

She nodded.

"Miss Croft, get him out of London. Plan on at least six months."

"That long?" She knew she was thinking only of herself, but the thought of not seeing Tynan for that long sincerely distressed her. She'd do it, of course. Her brother's life was at stake and that was far more important than her needs.

"It's your only chance to save him. Let me know where you decide to take him and I'll make arrangements with a doctor in the area to administer the dosage. In truth, I don't want you to take on this burden yourself. Your brother knows how to manipulate you. He'll rip your heart to shreds with his pleas for just a little more. He'll use your love for him as a weapon against you, because all that will matter to him is getting his hands on more opium."

She nibbled her lip. "I plan to get him out of here as soon as possible, but I don't have anywhere to take him yet."

Tynan squeezed her hand. "I'm making the arrangements this evening, Dr. Farthingale. Shall we meet here tomorrow morning? I'll give you the details then."

He nodded. "Of course, my lord. Once I know where you'll take him,

I'll give you the name of a trusted doctor to supervise his medication and recovery." He then turned to Abby. "I expect the travel arrangements will take several days to finalize. I'll come around twice a day in the meanwhile to look in on your brother and start his treatment."

"Thank you, yes." She worried about paying him for his services, but knew that Tynan intended to take on that obligation. She wouldn't fight him on the matter now since she had no funds at her disposal. But once her brother was better, she'd make certain that Tynan was repaid every shilling he was owed. "Is there anything I should do for Peter this evening?"

"Place a servant in his room to watch him through the night. Look in on him from time to time, if you wish. I don't think he'll be in any distress. In truth, he'll probably sleep the night away. But he'll be in discomfort by morning. I'll come to see him around nine o'clock."

"Thank you, doctor. I'll be waiting for you. I don't think I'll sleep a wink tonight."

After a few more words exchanged about travel arrangements between Dr. Farthingale and Tynan, the doctor left. She was now alone with Tynan, but he also appeared eager to leave. "Try to get some rest, Abby. We have a busy few days ahead of us."

We?

That sounded nice.

He surprised her with a gentle kiss on her cheek. "I shouldn't have done that, but I wanted to. Perhaps you do shatter my control."

She laughed and shook her head. "Ah, yes. I'm just that alluring, as you can tell by the horde of eligible young men pounding on my door."

"Lucky for me. I like having you all to myself." He tweaked her nose. "It's still pink. Just like a rabbit's."

CHAPTER SEVEN

TYNAN STEPPED OUT of his carriage later that evening into the Wicked Earls' Club that had become a second home to him, one that allowed him to indulge in all his vices. He gambled, at times. But that pastime was something he reverted to whenever he was not seducing some jaded noblewoman who was looking for a romp in the sack and no entanglements.

He misbehaved at will.

He discarded women with as much thought as he gave to discarding an unwanted playing card. They did the same, for this is how these Upper Crust games were played.

Until now, he'd enjoyed himself and given no thought to his future obligations.

But something had changed in him and Abby was squarely to blame. She was causing him to rethink the careless path of his life. There was no other logical reason for his sudden dissatisfaction with this indulgent part of his life. He hoped this change was temporary. "Good evening, m'lord," said the club's steward.

He nodded to the man, ignored the scantily clad women who tried to catch his eye as he strode past them, and headed toward the Earl of Coventry's office. To his relief, the earl had just arrived and was about to settle into the chair behind his desk with the club's ledger of accounts in front of him. "Ah, Westcliff. To what do I owe the pleasure?"

"I need a favor."

Coventry motioned for Tynan to shut the door and take a seat. "What is this about?"

Tynan sank into a chair across the desk from the man he'd come to think of as a father figure. He leaned forward, eager to have the conversation underway. "That young woman I rescued last night."

He proceeded to explain the situation to Coventry, careful to omit mention of that first kiss he'd shared with Abby. By the look Coventry was giving him, he'd probably guessed that more had passed between him and Abby than Tynan was letting on. Hell, that kiss had been mild compared to what he wished to do to the luscious girl. "You have a cottage in Falmouth that would suit Abby's... Miss Croft's needs perfectly. I'd like to lease it from you on her behalf."

Coventry leaned back in his chair and steepled his fingers under his chin as he considered all Tynan had told him and the request he'd made. "How often will you visit her?"

Tynan frowned. "Not often, if that's what has you concerned. Perhaps once a month. Sooner if she sends word to me that she needs my help. I'm not setting her up in a love nest. Her brother needs serious medical attention. Her time there will not be easy. In truth, I had hoped that you would escort her there. I don't want her associated with me. She needs privacy while dealing with her brother's situation, not her name emblazoned in headlines across the scandal sheets."

"I see. You're quite protective of the girl." He leaned forward and rested his elbows on his desk, his fingers still steepled under his chin as he contemplated his response. "What does she think of you?"

Tynan arched an eyebrow, at first considering a glib response, but Coventry deserved better. "She thinks of me as her savior."

"Hmm, her savior. I know the effect you have on women. She's probably in love with you by now."

"She's a careful girl." His chair squeaked as he shifted uncomfortably. "I doubt her thoughts are on anything other than saving her brother."

What was Coventry worried about? "Just tell me what's on your mind," he said, wanting to get back to Abby with good news about the arrangements as soon as possible. He'd told her that he'd see her tomorrow, but she'd invited him to stop by at any time if he had something to report, and he couldn't seem to get her out of his thoughts. He wanted to see her tonight.

"I heard from the staff of your good deed in saving Miss Croft. Now I understand what terrible business brought her here. She must have been desperate indeed to risk her life in coming after her brother. You do realize that she'll give you anything you ask because you are truly her savior, at least in her eyes."

"What's your point?"

"You are notorious in your dalliances with the ladies, Westcliff. How long before you come around to asking this young lady for the only thing that is hers to give you?"

He regarded Coventry, stunned. "I will not take her innocence against her will."

"I know, but you will take it because she won't be able to resist you."

Tynan's eyes began to blaze, more for the fact that Coventry was right about him and the likely outcome.

"You won't force her, I know that. Lying in your arms will probably be the best night of her life and she'll enjoy it. And then you'll be gone and she'll have nothing left of you... or of herself."

Tynan's jaw clenched and his entire body stiffened. "What are your terms?"

"I'll let the cottage in Falmouth to her and her brother for six months. I'll escort her there. I'll allow you to visit her because you are important to her, and I sense that she is important to you despite your disreputable ways. But if you take her innocence... you must promise to marry her."

He stared at Coventry, dumbfounded. "Marry her?"

Coventry's gaze was as sharp and piercing as that of a hawk's. "Do we have a deal?"

There were a thousand things Tynan wanted to say to the old man. There were a thousand curses he wanted to toss at him and a thousand refusals ready to spew from his lips. Instead, he said just one word. "Yes."

TYNAN KNEW HE was playing with fire by stopping by the Whitpool townhouse to look in on Abby and her brother one last time before he retired to his own bed... alone... in his own empty townhouse and not at his club.

He wasn't merely playing with fire but diving into it head first, especially after agreeing to suffer the direst of consequences if he ever seduced Abby. Surprisingly, that promise to marry her did not distress him nearly as much as he thought it would.

He glanced at his watch.

Almost eleven o'clock in the evening.

Had Abby retired to her quarters yet?

His carriage came to a halt outside her residence, but he did not immediately climb out. He looked for lights in the windows. There were several. One shone in Peter's bedchamber. Another shone in the drawing room, which meant Abby was still awake. "I won't be long," he told his driver.

After the promise he'd made to Coventry, he wasn't going to spend more time with the girl than necessary, not even to watch over Abby's brother.

Jameson was at the door, holding it open for him before he'd taken two steps through the gate. "Where is Miss Croft?"

Jameson pointed to the drawing room.

Tynan nodded. "Let her know that I wish to see her."

"Follow me, my lord. You may see her, but she's fallen asleep on the sofa. I dare not wake her. The poor thing hasn't had a decent night's sleep in weeks."

Tynan's breath caught in his chest the moment he entered and saw her slender form curled in a kittenish ball on the sofa. She'd unpinned her prettily upswept curls so that her glorious auburn hair was splayed across the blue silk decorative pillows.

She was in a deep, restful sleep. Her dark lashes rested upon her pale cheeks. Her pink lips were partly open and she was snoring in a soft, kittenish purr.

Lord help him, she was beautiful. Indeed, luminescent in the soft, golden firelight.

Someone had tucked a blanket over her shoulders rather than waken her. He was about to offer to carry her up to her bedchamber, but immediately decided against it. The girl was too tempting. "How is her brother faring?"

Jameson's eyes turned misty "Holding his own, my lord. At least for this evening. Vickers is sitting with him now. One of the footmen will take over from him in the morning."

Tynan nodded, but his gaze remained fixed on Abby. There was a purity to her beauty that he found fascinating and made it hard for him to draw his gaze away. "I'll come by with the doctor in the morning. Let her know that I stopped by with good news."

"I certainly will, my lord. She is in dire need of a reason to smile."

He nodded, taking a moment to brush a stray curl off her brow. Perhaps he only wanted a reason to touch her. She didn't wake up. He stifled his disappointment and leaned close. "Sweet dreams, Abby."

"You too, my dearest," she mumbled in her sleep.

Did she know she was speaking to him?

My dearest.

He'd received many endearments in his rakish life, but none had ever sounded sweeter. He rose and left her side, cursing himself with every stride. He shouldn't have come here tonight. He ought to have waited until morning. But he hadn't and his little rabbit, with her softly spoken words, had just taken another big bite out of him.

CHAPTER EIGHT

A MISSIVE CAME for Tynan the following morning, just as he was about to leave for the Whitpool residence. It was half past eight o'clock in the morning. Dr. Farthingale was due to visit there at nine, but Tynan hoped to arrive a few minutes earlier for a private word with Abby. He wanted to be sure that she was holding up all right and not quietly falling apart. Everyone, including Abby, had concentrated their attention on her brother.

Someone had to look out for her.

Why shouldn't it be him?

He stared at the paper in his hand, recognizing the seal embossed on it, and frowned. Coventry. What else did he want?

He unfolded the parchment to find nothing more than an invitation to join him for tea at the Coventry residence. The invitation included a request to bring Abby with him. He nodded his approval, for that made sense. The three of them would need to review the details of her travel plans to Falmouth and the terms of her stay at Coventry's cottage.

Of course, an earl's cottage was no unassuming two room house with an aging thatched roof. Although Tynan had never seen the property, he expected the house to be a stately manor constructed of brick or local stone and containing at least twenty rooms. Those would include two or three dining rooms, a music room, a library, the earl's study, two parlors, and no less than six or seven bedchambers.

He tucked the missive in his breast pocket, pleased with the speed at which matters were progressing.

Abby met him at the Whitpool front door, her brandy eyes wide and sparkling, and a heartwarming smile on her soft lips. Her woolen gown was the auburn color of her hair, and as usual, she had little adornment other than a bit of lace trim at her collar and the cuffs of her sleeves.

"Jameson said you had good news to tell me. I'm so sorry I wasn't awake to see you last night. Did you sleep well? You look wonderful. But don't you always?"

He was a jaded, cynical earl, so how did she manage to send his heart careening every time he set eyes on her? "I think you will find it is very good news."

He laughed when she suddenly took him by the forearm and dragged him into the drawing room. He understood that she was excited to hear of the plans for her brother's recovery. "Tell me everything, Tynan. I'm so grateful. You've brought me yet another miracle. Oh, dear. Have you had a bite to eat yet? May I offer you–"

"Abby, I'm fine. Calm down and let me tell you what I've arranged. But first, tell me how your brother is faring."

Her smile faltered a little. "He's survived the night and is sleeping restfully."

"Good." He settled on the sofa and was pleased when she took a seat beside him. Since she was leaping out of her skin to hear the details, he wasted no more time on pleasantries. "The Earl of Coventry has agreed to help you."

"Thank you, Tynan," she said with such breathless ardor, one would think he'd just given her a necklace of diamonds. But to Abby, the means to save her brother was far more precious than any dazzling gemstone.

"The earl has a house in Falmouth that he will let to you for six months, or longer should the need arise. He'll send word today to his housekeeper to have the house readied for your arrival and intends to accompany you there. But he can't leave until the end of the week, so it will be another five or six days until you are underway."

She listened intently and nodded as he set forth the details.

He felt the light curl of her fingers against his own. Somehow, she'd taken hold of his hand.

Or had he taken hers?

He supposed it didn't matter, for their hands were entwined and neither one of them had any desire to let go.

He knew they shouldn't be holding hands at all. He knew that he shouldn't have kissed her yesterday. He was playing with fire by being here now, caring about this girl, and willing to move heaven and earth to help her.

He knew that he shouldn't want to kiss her again, but he did want to and probably would kiss her because she was becoming a craving for him.

Hell, merely holding her hand was twisting him inside out.

He wasn't going to release her, nor was he going to think about what was happening between them. He liked the way she made him feel. But everything could change tomorrow. He was a disreputable rogue and his feelings weren't to be trusted.

He cleared his throat. "Coventry has invited us to tea at his residence this afternoon. I expect it will be just the three of us, perhaps his wife and one of his trusted clerks, too. We'll need to work out the details of your stay and this is as good a time as any for you to get to know the Earl of Coventry. I'm sure he's eager to meet you."

"Tynan," she said with a sweet ache to her voice, "thank you a thousand times over."

He saw that she was getting sentimental and quickly sought to change the topic before he took her into his arms to soothe her. Of course, holding her in his arms would have the opposite effect on him, leaving him in fiery torment. Which would lead to more kisses, none of which would be tame or remotely proper.

He released her hand and stood, needing to put a little distance between him and Abby. "Shall we look in on Peter?"

"Not yet. Let's wait for the doctor. My brother is sleeping peacefully and I wouldn't like to disturb him. He was snoring when I tiptoed in earlier this morning." She took a deep breath. "He was alive. He *is* alive."

She appeared ready to say more, but rose instead and moved toward the window as a carriage clattered to a stop in front of her home. "Oh, excellent. Dr. Farthingale is here."

Although she stood quietly and appeared calm, Tynan saw that her fingers were nervously playing with the lace on her collar. "Abby, he's the best. If anyone can heal your brother, it's Dr. Farthingale."

She nodded. "I knew he had to be the best because you brought him to me. He put me at ease the moment I met him. You keep performing these miracles for me, Tynan. I... there's too much I want to say to you... and I keep praying that I won't ever lose you, which is ridiculous because it will happen. It's just a question of when."

"Abby, you exaggerate my importance." He didn't know what else to say.

She cast him the sweetest smile. "Not at all. Meeting you has been a precious gift for me. I may think of you as my angel, but I know you are very much a man of flesh and blood, with strengths and weaknesses as we all have. I know we will part ways, certainly once my brother and I ride off to Falmouth. But I also want you to know that I shall never forget you and all you've done for me."

Jameson announced the doctor, sparing Tynan the need of a reply. He didn't know what to say to Abby. Yes, he would leave. That's what men like him did.

After briefly telling the doctor about the travel plans he'd arranged with Coventry, he followed Abby and the doctor upstairs to her brother's chamber. "I know of an excellent man in Falmouth," Dr. Farthingale said as they climbed the stairs. "I'll write to him to let him know the situation and to expect Miss Croft or Lord Coventry to contact him upon their arrival."

Abby graced the doctor with one of her generous smiles. "That sounds perfect."

They entered Peter's chamber. Tynan stood quietly beside Abby, his arms folded across his chest as the doctor checked Peter's pulse, his heartbeat, and set his hand across his brow to check for fever.

Tynan knew that Abby's brother was still fighting off a fever, for his complexion was sallow, except for his cheeks that were stained a bright pink, and he was shivering while, at the same time, his hair and forehead were soaked in sweat.

Abby began to fuss again with the lace at her collar. She'd noticed her brother's condition, too. The fact that he appeared to be sleeping peacefully was no cause for rejoicing. In truth, as the drugs wore off, he should have been tossing and turning and grumbling. But he wasn't, for the bad mix of drugs and fever were sapping the life from him. "Peter, the doctor is here. Open your eyes, my dearest. How do you feel?"

My dearest.

Tynan stifled his disappointment, realizing she'd thought he was Peter wishing her sweet dreams last night.

She hadn't been responding to him at all, but to her brother.

Whatever disappointment he might have felt disappeared a moment later as Peter stirred awake and realized that he was being guarded.

"Damn you, Abby. Get the hell out of here," he snarled, and then began to hurl curses at her that made even Tynan blush. Each vile epithet was like a punch to Abby's heart, for the girl wore her heart on her sleeve and Tynan noticed the subtle recoil of her body with each blow Peter landed.

Heat flooded Abby's cheeks and tears welled in her eyes.

Tynan put a protective arm around her, but it wasn't enough to lend comfort. She had to be so deeply hurt by this brother who didn't deserve her love. Was this the same man who'd uttered "I love you" to his sister only yesterday?

Dr. Farthingale exchanged a pitying glance with him. "My lord, would you escort Miss Croft downstairs?"

Since Tynan already had his hands on her trembling shoulders, he nodded and steered her out. "Come along, Abby."

Had her brother not been at death's door, Tynan would have taken his fists to him. The man deserved to have the stuffing beat out of him. He hated that Abby had to endure this treatment. "I know he doesn't mean it," she said as they descended the stairs. "He's sick and doesn't know what he's saying."

"Come with me. We're going for a walk in the park. You need to get out of here for a while."

"But the doctor—"

"He'll wait for us to return. We won't be long." He called for Jameson to fetch Abby's cloak.

"What about the need for discretion? You and me alone? It isn't proper. We'll draw everyone's attention."

The girl had almost been killed two days ago and had seen her brother almost die yesterday. She had endured being savagely cursed out by the wretch only moments ago. And she was worried about taking a walk in the park with him? He shook his head and sighed. "Your maid can follow us."

"But the *ton* gossips will see us together."

"My carriage is standing outside your front door, the Westcliff crest on prominent display. Every one of your neighbors has noticed that I've come around two days in a row now. It's done, Abby. I'm not going to squirrel you away. You're not my mistress or some indiscreet liaison that I need to hide from prying eyes."

She frowned at him. "Then they'll think you're courting me."

"So what?" In truth, he was no longer afraid to let their acquaintance take whatever course it was meant to take. He would be honest with Abby. She'd know the truth, whatever that truth was. "Are you ashamed to be seen with me?"

"No! Of course not." She appeared genuinely surprised, and her eyes rounded in horror. "I should think it is the other way around, that you don't wish to be seen with me."

"I'm not objecting, so why should you?"

"But... I..." She shook her head and sighed. "Very well, I suppose I'd rather be respectably jilted than be considered a hidden mistress that you've ruined and abandoned." She squared her shoulders and cast him a surprisingly innocent and earnest gaze. "But if the gossip does ruin me,

I'm not going to let it be in vain."

"What do you mean?"

"If I am ruined..." She paused to take a deep breath which she then released with a light groan. "If I am..."

"Ruined?"

She nodded and her cheeks took on a bright, pink glow. "Then I'd like to spend it productively... with you, and... and that peacock feather. I'd love to find out what you do with it. I'm quite intrigued and cannot imagine its purpose. Will you promise me—"

"No!"

Mother in heaven.

"Heaven ought to protect rakehells from innocent young women like you," he muttered, his entire body catching fire.

She eyed him with confusion. "Don't you mean it the other way around?"

"No. Stop chattering and come along."

Although it was too early for most of the *ton* to be up and about, there were enough gentlemen and ladies strolling through the park at this late hour of the morning that he and Abby did not seem out of place. In addition, there were plenty of riders along Rotten Row, and children guarded by their nannies playing beside the Serpentine.

He and Abby drew attention because everyone knew who Tynan was, but no one dared approach without his permission which he did not grant. He could not recall ever escorting a young lady through the park before.

He never took genteel walks.

He glanced about, regarding the scenery with a cynical eye. Until this moment, these trees and surrounding shrubbery would have represented locations for seduction, hidden spots where he could take a willing lady for the purpose of a quick tumble before anyone – often a husband – noticed she was missing. Gardens served the same purpose, for there were lots of secluded alcoves where sunlight did not reach.

He shook out of his thoughts, suddenly not liking himself very much. This is what his life had been until Abby came along. He wasn't a complete scoundrel, for he never seduced innocents, but he was still a wretched reprobate in many ways.

He found it odd that Abby seemed to bring out the better part of him. She walked beside him, unaware of what he was thinking. He liked having her beside him and was determined to behave himself around her, no matter how difficult she made it for him. She deserved to be treated like a princess, not like the whipping post her brother had used her for only moments ago. And not like some meaningless sexual escapade for him. "How do you feel, Abby? A little better, I hope."

She nodded. "It's a beautiful day. I love the warmth of the sun on my face and the cool, gentle wind in my hair."

He'd been in such a rush to get her out of that house, he hadn't given her time to put on a bonnet. But she didn't seem to mind, nor did he. Her auburn hair was a fiery, dark brown that glistened in the sunshine, the deep reds and earthy browns caught in the shifting light depending on the tilt of her head.

The sky was a deep, clear blue and the sun was gently beating down on them. Tynan even heard birds chirping in the trees. He noticed the vivid reds and yellows of the changing leaves. The brilliant colors struck him all at once, the azure blue of the sky, the fiery reds and golds of the falling leaves, the white puffs of clouds. But nothing was as beautiful as Abby's auburn hair and auburn gown and her smiling brandy eyes.

Abby closed her eyes and tilted her head upward to soak in the warmth of the sun. She looked even lovelier in the morning light than she had by the glow of firelight. Hell, she looked spectacular either way. "Thank you, Tynan. I did need this moment of peace."

"Any time, Abby. I'm entirely at your disposal."

She laughed and opened her eyes as they resumed walking. "I won't hold you to your words. But I do enjoy your company. It isn't every day I have a handsome earl willing to indulge my every whim."

"I'm not indulging you. If I am, it's quite a tame indulgence."

She smiled up at him. "Ah, I almost forgot. Your indulgences include peacock feathers and black ribbons. I'm particularly fascinated by the peacock feather–"

He shook his head and groaned. "I noticed."

"And I am determined to discover what depraved purpose you use it for."

He growled softly. "Stop bringing it up or else I will show you, mercilessly and deliciously, until your body sings for me… only me."

He shouldn't have said that, but her innocent curiosity fascinated him as much as that damn feather fascinated her. He loved the way her cheeks suddenly turned crimson and her eyes widened in lurid surprise.

She laughed instead of berating him.

He liked that Abby was innocent, but not a prude.

There was a hidden naughty side to her that no man had yet drawn out. The possessive part of him wanted to be the first to teach her about lovemaking, and that same possessive part of him wanted to be the only man ever to make love to her. She was his.

I'm the wolf. She's my rabbit.

Bollocks.

When had he turned into a blithering idiot?

He'd given his word to Coventry. He'd have to marry her if he ever touched her like that. Yet, that dire outcome did nothing to diminish his desire for the girl. She had a way of twisting him inside out. How ironic that she should wield such power over him when she had no idea what she was doing. "But the purpose of the peacock feather isn't depraved. Perhaps improper, but that's all."

"It sounds utterly and completely depraved," she said, but he saw the curiosity in her eyes and knew she wasn't nearly as shocked as she pretended to be.

He stopped walking and tucked a finger under her chin, tipping her head upward to meet his gaze. He grinned wickedly. "You don't know what you're talking about. Let me explain it to you in a way your innocent mind will understand. There is a distinct and important difference between the terms *improper* and *depraved*. Using a peacock feather to enhance sexual arousal is *improper*. Having sex with the peacock is *depraved*."

She stared at him. "And you only use the feather?"

Lord, help him!

Did she think he kept a barnyard in his bedchamber?

"Yes, only the feather. I do not take animals into my bed."

Bollocks.

How had their conversation spiraled so completely out of control? He'd brought her to the park to ease her mind, not fill it with indecent conversation. He was about to apologize, when she suddenly giggled.

The giggles soon turned into hearty laughter. "I do believe that *W* on your lapel pin stands for 'wicked' not 'Westcliff'."

"Ah, you've found me out." In truth, she had. The W was the discreet pin worn by members of the Wicked Earls' Club. It was mere coincidence that his title happened to be Westcliff and started with a *W*.

Her laughter faded, but she was still smiling and her eyes were still gleaming with mirth. "Perhaps that W stands for wonderful, too. That's how you made me feel just now, Tynan. My brother's words hurt me so deeply, I think I needed this bit of silliness to remind me not to despair."

He raked a hand through his hair. "Abby, don't make me out to be heroic. I'm not."

Her smile turned wistful. "You needn't worry about my holding any illusions about you. I see you clearly for what you are… peacock feathers and all."

He laughed.

This was one of the things he liked about Abby. He could tease her, be playfully outrageous with her, and she took it all in good nature. There was no mock prudery or false indignation about her. No doubt she'd developed her resilience by growing up with four brothers. That she was so young and had already lost three of them should have left her bitter and angry.

Instead, it had made her strong and compassionate.

"We had better return home," she said, now glancing around to make certain they hadn't attracted too much attention. "I don't want to keep Dr. Farthingale waiting. I hope he's calmed my brother."

They turned back and entered the Whitpool townhouse a few moments before the doctor descended the stairs. "Miss Croft, I'll return in the early evening. Your brother is still running a fever, but it is abating. Keep a close watch on him, especially as he improves. He'll want to return to his opium club as soon as he finds the strength to climb out of bed."

She nodded. "My staff is taking turns guarding him."

"And I've hired Bow Street runners to watch this house," Tynan added.

Abby turned to him in surprise. "You have?"

He nodded, knowing he ought to have mentioned it sooner, but he could see her calculating the cost of everything he offered, and didn't want her worrying about all she believed she owed him. He would not accept repayment from her, but he wasn't going to have that fight with her now. "They start this evening."

Since he intended to escort Abby to Lord Coventry's home in a few hours, he decided to spend the rest of the day with her, accompanying her on her morning errands. She needed to prepare for an extended journey and had only a few days in which to ready herself and her brother. It was agreed that her maid, Sally, would serve as her chaperone. While the situation wasn't perfect, the maid's watchful presence was enough to lend propriety to their outing.

Tongues would wag, but no permanent damage would be done. It could not be said that Abby had gone around town with him unsupervised.

"Where shall we stop first?" he asked, admiring her organizational skills. She made lists for herself and for her brother. She carefully mapped out their route so that there was no time lost going from shop to shop, and was genuinely appreciative when he offered to cut the chores in half by taking on the task of shopping for her brother.

"Are you certain you don't mind, Lord Westcliff?" she asked, addressing him formally while they were in the company of Sally.

"Not at all," he replied, surprised that he did not feel imposed upon.

He found it easy to be with Abby, enjoyed her smiles of delight and the fact that she made no demands on him. She was obviously relieved that he was willing to help, and at the same time would have been as understanding if he'd refused to assist her.

While she made stops at her modiste and milliner, he went to the men's shops on Regent Street.

They met up again at one o'clock, having made inroads in their list of chores. After stopping at her home to drop off their purchases, they rode to Lord Coventry's residence.

Tynan hadn't felt so at ease in years.

He was almost gleeful by the time they were admitted into Coventry's expansive home, for he was quite proud of Abby and looked forward to introducing her to the old earl. But all his good humor fled the moment they were shown into the drawing room. "Bastard," Tynan muttered under his breath. "I should have known he'd pull something like this."

Abby regarded him with concern. "What's wrong? Who are these people? And why are they gawking at me?"

CHAPTER NINE

"THAT TALL WOMAN with the blindingly bright red hair who is grinning at you and appears about to suffocate you in her bosom... is my mother," Tynan grumbled, standing at the entrance to Coventry's drawing room and holding Abby back as though protecting her from hungry wolves. Well, perhaps it was a bit of an exaggeration.

Abby's gorgeous brandy eyes widened. "You have a mother?"

He nodded. "Someone had to spawn me. She's the culprit."

Abby laughed and shook her head. "Then I will make it a point to thank her. It never occurred to me that you might have parents, but of course you must. You didn't simply descend from the heavens. Do you know the others?"

"Yes. All of them, unfortunately." Coventry, the wily, old fox, had not only invited – *Lord, help him* – his mother, but his brothers as well. He looked beyond the three, giant specimens who were his irritating brothers and saw more Brayden relatives. "In fact, I couldn't get rid of the lot of them even if I wanted to. They're my family."

She gasped and put a hand to her throat. "How lovely. Tynan, you're so fortunate. I wish..."

She clamped her lips shut, but he knew that she was wishing for a big, loving family of her own. She was desperate for it, he could see it in the bright glow of her eyes.

He didn't respond to her remark, for he knew that he ought to be grateful. In truth, he was, even though he rarely showed it. Abby, a girl with so much love in her heart that it spilled out of every pore of her beautiful body, had lost almost everyone she loved. She ached for exactly the family he had and would never have taken them for granted as he was doing. Indeed, he knew that he ought to have been a better son, a better brother, but at times, he found his responsibilities toward them suffocating.

What had possessed Coventry to invite them? He liked the old man, but he was going to kill him for this hoax.

James and Sophie were also present, to his relief. Sophie immediately rushed forward to greet Abby. "Come, meet Tynan's mother," she said with a gentle laugh, taking Abby's hand and drawing her away from him. "His brothers as well."

Abby turned back to him, her eyes gleaming with mirth. Apparently, everyone thought this turn of events hilarious. "Oh, Tynan. You look as though your heart has just stopped. Don't fret. I'm delighted to meet them all."

Sophie gave a snorting chortle. "I've never seen you at a loss for words before, Ty."

Well, he was at a loss. He didn't want his closest blood relations here. He no longer wished to be here himself. And he certainly did not want Abby getting too friendly with any of them. He wasn't ashamed of her, but he would not have his family believing that he was about to mend his rakehell ways.

Coventry stepped forward and took Abby in an effusive hug. "Welcome, my dear."

Abby cast the old hound a heartwarming smile when he released her. "Thank you for inviting me into your home, Lord Coventry. And for your generous assistance."

Tynan growled.

Abby shook her head and laughed again softly. "Lord Westcliff is still fuming, I fear. It is not well done of you to surprise him like this, my lord. But I think you and I shall get along quite well, for I see you have a wicked sense of humor and I have a desperate need for laughter in my life."

She glanced at Tynan, obviously wishing for him to get over this unpleasant surprise and be the one to introduce her to his family. He'd rather descend into the pits of hell. Why was his family here? And how quickly could he get rid of them?

"You ought to have warned me of your intention," Tynan said, curling his fists at his sides and still scowling at Coventry. Yes, the old earl was a dead man, he just didn't know it yet.

Coventry wasn't in the least intimidated. "And deprive your family of the pleasure of meeting Miss Croft? May I call you Abigail? Yes, I shall do so, I think." He now turned away from Tynan and spoke directly to Abby. "You've been seen around town with this wicked earl. He seems to think the presence of your maid is sufficient to protect your good name, but I know better. Nothing less than his family's support and approval will do."

Tynan sighed in surrender. "Bollocks, keep away from her, Coventry. I can see already that you'll be a bad influence. I'll introduce Abigail to my family."

He felt like a fly trapped in a spider's web. Struggling to escape was useless. He placed Abby's hand on his forearm and led her to his mother. "Lady Miranda Grayfell, the woman solely to blame for the way I turned out," he said, his humor returning now that he'd resigned himself to his fate. "And these giant nuisances are my brothers, Ronan, Joshua, and Finn. And this last young giant, is Romulus. He's also a Brayden."

"He's my baby brother," James said, setting aside his cane to give her a warm greeting. "We have more siblings and aunts and... well, Coventry didn't want to overwhelm you. The Braydens are a large family."

"In more ways than one," Abby remarked, gazing up at all of them.

Sophie moved to her side. "Yes, they're as big as gladiators, aren't they? But I have no doubt you'll hold your own against them. I'm glad you're here. Now I won't be the only runt of the litter."

Abby and Sophie were of average height, but the Brayden men and women were tall, no doubt because a few Vikings had plundered their bloodline in the early centuries.

Abby's eyes grew misty.

He understood what she was thinking. The Braydens could have resembled her family had her own brothers survived. Her hand was still resting on his forearm. When he felt her shiver, he settled his other hand over hers. "Abby?"

"I'm all right. A little overwhelmed, but in the nicest way." She turned to his mother and declined the handkerchief she was offering. "Lady Miranda, you've raised a wonderful son."

His mother arched an eyebrow. "I have?"

Abby nodded. "The best. You ought to be very proud of him."

His brothers made gagging sounds.

Ah, nothing like brothers to keep a man humble. He grabbed Joshua and Finn by the scruff of their necks and motioned for Ronan and Romulus to follow him. They were still young, not yet through with university, except for Ronan who had graduated a few months ago – shockingly, with honors – and was now helping him with the Westcliff family enterprises.

Still, all of them were in the midst of sowing their wild oats and could not be trusted to be discreet. The discussion about Abby's situation was not for their young ears. "Get lost until tea is served. Go play billiards. Or go jump in Coventry's ridiculously oversized fountain. Or read a book. Can any of you read?"

The boys took off like a stampeding herd of elephants.

They were familiar with the Coventry residence, for the old earl and his countess were good friends and as close to the Brayden family as anyone could be.

But Tynan was still going to kill Coventry for bringing his mother here. His mother!

And now she and Sophie and Lady Coventry were fawning over Abby.

Damn it, his mother's smile was as bright as a sunbeam.

Coventry came up to him and began to speak quietly. "I'm sorry, my boy. I know I went about this in a heavy-handed manner. But I was only thinking of Abby. You wish to protect her, don't you?"

Tynan's jaw had been clenched, and his response came out clipped and tense. "Of course."

"Then let your family help. They need do nothing more than welcome her as a friend."

Tynan grunted. "That's already been accomplished. Didn't take long. Sophie looks upon her like a long lost sister. Look at my mother, she's already halfway in love with her."

Coventry place a hand on his shoulder. "And what about you, Tynan? How do you feel about the girl?"

He shot Coventry a scowl and walked away.

Hell, he was a wicked earl.

He wasn't some pimple-arsed schoolboy who fell in love with anything in skirts.

He was cynical and experienced and never one to be led around by the nose.

And yet… it was as though this girl had found the big, gaping hole in his defenses and leaped straight through.

Abby, his innocent little rabbit, was burrowing her way into his heart.

He didn't know how to stop her.

Or if he wanted to stop her.

CHAPTER TEN

"LORD WESTCLIFF, I'D give anything for a family like yours," Abby said once the tea was over and Tynan was taking her home in his carriage. Sally sat with them, so Abby was careful not to speak of anything too personal. But heaping praise on his family wasn't too much, was it? "They are simply wonderful. I know that you did not expect them to be present, but I really enjoyed my time in their company."

He grunted.

She smiled at him.

He frowned at her, but couldn't hide the hint of a smile twitching at the corners of his nicely shaped lips.

He obviously loved his family, but he was purposely keeping his distance from them and had done so for several years. Abby was curious to know the reason, for they all appeared to get along. She hadn't heard of any dark secrets or simmering feuds. His brothers and Romulus were out of hand, at times. But they were still young men at that stage in their lives when they wanted independence but were too immature to handle it. "How old were you when you took over responsibilities as earl?"

At first, she thought he wouldn't answer.

She did not press him for a response, and thought he'd forgotten the question by the time they arrived at her home. Sally took their cloaks and then left them to their privacy. Abby's first thought was to look in on Peter. "Do you mind, Tynan?"

"Not at all. I'll join you."

She knocked softly on Peter's door and was relieved when it quickly opened. "Vickers, how is he?"

"Hanging on, Miss Abigail. He's been quiet ever since that nasty dustup this morning."

She breathed a sigh and then tiptoed to his bed, needing to see him, even if only for a moment. Once satisfied that her brother was not in any distress, she ushered Tynan into the drawing room. "Would you care for a glass of port while we wait for Dr. Farthingale? He should be stopping by soon. Unless you've had enough of all of us and wish to leave. I'd certainly understand."

He cast her a wry grin. "I'm not tired of you, Abby. It's everyone else I wish would disappear."

She shook her head in confusion as she settled on the sofa and watched him stride across the room to pour himself a glass of the deep ruby-colored spirits. "Why do you wish everyone else would disappear?"

This was another question she didn't expect him to answer, but to her surprise, he settled beside her, unfastened the buttons of his jacket, and stretched his legs before him. "I took over responsibility for managing the earldom of Westcliff almost a decade ago."

"A decade ago? You must have been younger than me at the time."

He nodded. "The title itself descended to me from my uncle only a few months ago, upon my uncle's death. But he was sickly for most of his adult life, and he and his wife were never able to have children. The responsibility would have fallen upon my father, but he passed away when I was eighteen. That's when I became Viscount Grayfell, inheriting my father's title."

She listened, fascinated and a little surprised that he was confiding in her. Well, the matter of his father's death as well as that of his uncle's was public knowledge. But there was an intimacy in the way he spoke to her, and she cherished earning his trust.

"For the past decade, I've been managing the Westcliff and Grayfell holdings, and stepping in to help my mother raise my younger brothers whenever the need arose."

Abby smiled. "They are a handful. I imagine you had to step in quite often in their younger years."

He nodded. "I did, but Lord Coventry helped enormously. He saw that I was taking on more than a young man could handle, especially with my brothers, and especially while trying to make my own way through university while at the same time managing the family business affairs. He stepped in and helped me out. Most gentlemen of my age were going to balls and dinner parties and the theater, but I spent most of my earlier years trying to keep my brothers from killing each other, studying for exams, and working to turn a profit on our lands and businesses."

She regarded him, confused. "When did you have the time to earn your sordid reputation?"

"Sordid? I prefer to think of it as rakish."

She laughed. "Very well, rakish reputation."

He shrugged. "Obviously not back then. I had the family obligations on my shoulders. But I was curious to find out what I'd been missing all these years. Once I had the businesses sufficiently well established and turning a profit, and my brothers were old enough to be left on their own without fear they'd burn down the manor house, I left them in my mother's capable care and came to London to enjoy all the temptations this lively town offered."

"I understand. You were like a coiled spring finally unwinding." She tucked her legs under her and rested her arms on the sofa's firm back. "I feel that way sometimes. But I don't have any rakish desires." She cast him an impish grin. "Other than a mild curiosity about peacock feathers."

"Abby." He rolled his eyes in obvious exasperation.

She held up her hands and laughingly shook her head. "I know. Sorry. I won't raise it again, but I couldn't help tweaking you about it. Don't be angry with me, Tynan. I haven't been so happy in an afternoon for such a long time. I miss what your family gave me today, the joyful chaos of a caring family. It warmed my heart as nothing else could. I hope to have that someday. I know it won't happen before Peter is healthy again, but it's all right. I can wait."

He drained his glass and set it aside. "Abby, would you mind if I left before Dr. Farthingale arrives?"

"I think I've imposed on you more than enough for one day." She smiled at him, hoping she hid her disappointment well. "Please don't feel obligated to wait for him. Shall I let you know if he mentions something important? I doubt he will. I think he has my brother's treatment well in hand."

"Send word to me at my townhouse if anything urgent does come up. I mean it, Abby. You won't be imposing on me." He rose and stretched his muscled back. "I'll see you tomorrow morning."

"Truly?" She rose along with him to see him out, her heart beating a little faster at the prospect she'd see him again. While she appreciated all Lord Coventry had agreed to do for her and her brother, there was no doubt that he'd badly overstepped this afternoon and made Tynan feel more than a little uncomfortable. Lord Coventry had said he'd done it to protect her reputation, but she was growing to care more for Tynan's happiness than any possible taint to her name.

Tynan had held his anger in check, but she knew that he was still quietly seething and needed to be away from her in order to release his anger. It was no business of hers what he did next, and she appreciated that he did not wish to show her a lesser side of him… assuming he had one.

She thought of him as her savior.

He didn't want to tarnish that illusion.

But she understood that his pent up frustration had to be let out. She didn't know what he was going to do this evening. It wasn't her place to ask. Nor did she wish to think about him in the arms of another woman. She wanted to be the one he took into his arms, but it wasn't going to happen.

She was still innocent, and this big, handsome, wicked earl did not defile innocents.

He cupped her cheek in his big, rough hand, his touch exquisitely gentle. "Yes, Abby. I will come by tomorrow. We've only gone through a quarter of your list. So, plan our route and make your efficiently precise lists. I'll come around at eleven o'clock in the morning. Does that suit you?"

She nodded. "That suits me very well."

She felt bereft when he slipped his hand off her face, so desperate for more of his touch. She thought for a moment that he'd kiss her, but he was already in the entry hall and about to walk out the door.

Within a matter of days, she'd be on her way to Falmouth and he'd be out of her life.

Please remember me, Tynan. Please.

TYNAN STROLLED INTO the Wicked Earls' Club and immediately began to wonder why he'd bothered to come by this evening. But he knew why. He was thinking of Abby to the point of obsession and needed something to distract his mind. Ever since meeting her, she'd not only captured his attention, but somehow held him hostage to her charms, ones she had no idea she had and no idea how to use.

She consumed his thoughts.

He shuddered to think what power she'd hold over him once she learned how to use her charms to greatest effect.

He supposed this was what troubled him most. Until Abby had come along, he'd always held the power in relations with women. He'd always wielded the control.

Not with Abby.

Yet, he wasn't powerless over her. He knew that she liked him and was so desperate for love, that she would surrender herself to him, heart and soul, with very little effort on his part. She would be a joy to take into his bed, for she was innocent and eager, and delightfully intrigued by that peacock feather. "No, can't bed her."

He'd promised Coventry.

Taking her into his bed would mean having to marry her.

Bollocks.

He still felt not a hint of panic at the prospect.

Which meant he must be feverish and on the brink of delirium.

Coventry happened to walk out of his office just then. "What's wrong, Westcliff? Not feeling well?"

Tynan dropped his hand from his forehead because he wasn't ill. His forehead was cool to the touch and he had no convenient excuse to explain his fascination with Abby. "I'm fine," he grumbled. "I was looking for the viscountess. A little unfinished business that Abby interrupted on the night we met."

Coventry tossed him a sour look. "You're going to pursue the viscountess?"

What troubled Tynan most was the look of disappointment on the old man's face. He'd rather have his mentor angry and shouting at him. But Coventry was casting him that patient, 'you know you're a better man than this' look and Tynan suddenly felt like an ungrateful child. "Yes, I'm going to pursue her. She's safe. Married. The sex is meaningless."

"And you're willing to settle for that?"

Now Tynan was getting angry. "I'd pursue Abby, but you set down the rules. If I bed her, I marry her. And you know damn well that a night spent with Abby would never be meaningless to–" He turned away and raked a hand through his hair. "I don't owe Abby or you any explanations."

"Indeed, you don't." Coventry had a smug look on his face. "So why do you keep mentioning her?"

"Me?" Tynan shook his head and laughed. "You're the one who keeps..." Hell, the old man was right. Coventry had never once mentioned the girl. "I'm going home. This club is getting boring."

He marched out and called for his carriage. The night was still young. His mother was hosting a musicale and had begged him to make an appearance. He got hives just thinking of it. Since he had nothing better to do, he decided to call on Abby.

Coventry planned to escort them to Falmouth on the day after tomorrow. He could resist her charms until then, couldn't he?

Besides, he enjoyed the time he spent with the girl.

He'd miss her once she was gone.

Bollocks.

No, he wouldn't... he just had to keep telling himself that.

He climbed out the moment his carriage rolled to a stop in front of her house. Her ever efficient butler, Jameson, was at the door with hands outstretched to take his cloak. To Tynan's surprise, the man looked visibly upset. "What's wrong? Where's Abby?"

Drat! He ought to have referred to her as Miss Croft or Miss Abigail, but the thought of something dire happening to her... and that he hadn't been there to help her, troubled him.

"She's in her bedchamber, my lord. I don't think she'll wish to see you."

He arched an eyebrow in surprise. "Why not?"

"We all let down our defenses. Things seemed to be going so well these past few days."

Tynan's heart shot into his throat. "Jameson, tell me what happened."

"We wanted to send word to you, but Miss Abigail wouldn't allow it." His expression crumbled. "Her brother accidentally struck her. She's nursing a cut lip."

Tynan took the stairs two at a time, pausing only a moment to knock at Abby's door before he stormed in without invitation. She was seated on a stool beside the hearth, a handkerchief pressed to one corner of her mouth and tears streaming down her cheeks. "Oh, Abby," he said with an agonized groan, "why didn't you summon me?"

She turned away, obviously unwilling to face him. "You were busy. I've imposed on you so much already. This is just more of the same with Peter. He wants his opium and I won't give it to him."

She looked so vulnerable and yet so determined to press on alone. And why shouldn't she? He was so damn busy trying to deny his feelings for her, trying to preserve his distance, his power and control, that he'd made certain to set rigid boundaries between them. Ones he would not cross and ones he would not give her permission to cross.

He was a horse's arse.

He knelt beside her and tilted her face toward his, examining her lip by firelight. To his relief, it wasn't cut. It wasn't even badly bruised. Her brother must have dealt her a glancing blow, the surprise of it more shocking than the actual damage. Indeed, the swelling was hardly noticeable. Perhaps Peter had meant to strike her harder, but he hadn't the strength yet.

What would happen when he regained his strength at Falmouth?

Tynan ran his thumb gently across the swollen corner of her mouth. "Does it hurt badly?"

"Not when you touch me." She rubbed the sleeve of her gown against her cheeks to wipe away her tears.

He gave her a short, feather-soft kiss on the mouth.

She cast him a hesitant smile. "That doesn't hurt either. You could never hurt me, Tynan."

She was wrong.

He'd never physically hurt her, but he had it in his power to crush her soul. She was so vulnerable, it would take nothing for her to fall in love with him. He saw it in the dark amber glow of her eyes.

He felt her loneliness and her yearning ache for love.

He shouldn't have come here. Yet, he wasn't about to walk out and leave her alone to her obvious misery. "Abby, my mother is hosting a musicale this evening. Will you allow me to escort you there?"

Her eyes rounded in surprise. "Oh, no. I couldn't."

He touched her lip with exquisite care again. "No one will notice the light swelling. Your lips have a natural lushness and a rose tinge to them that will hide any damage." He grinned tenderly. "My mother will think I was avidly kissing you. You will only enhance my wicked reputation."

She laughed. "Oh, Tynan. I know you find these entertainments deadly dull. You've made no secret of it."

"But you like them, don't you?"

"Yes." She nodded reluctantly. "You needn't worry about me. I'll be just as content to curl up on my sofa with a good book to read."

"Come with me, Abby." He brushed a stray curl off her forehead. "You've been alone too long. Tomorrow is our last day together. I won't see you for at least another month afterward. So, take pity on this wicked earl."

"I think it is the other way around, you taking pity on me. But I would like to go. Very much. If you really don't mind."

Her eyes were big and hopeful once again as she sought confirmation in his expression. "I want you with me, Abby. In truth, I need to get you out of here before I lose my control and beat the stuffing out of your brother. I know he's going through a hard time. I know he loves you. But it doesn't excuse his cruel treatment of you." He sighed and shook his head, suddenly wanting to offer this girl everything.

She'd called her brother, that undeserving wretch, *my dearest*. She'd nursed her brother through his addiction, through raging fever, and had never once complained.

No one looked out for her.

In truth, she was holding up admirably on her own.

But he couldn't leave her now. He was going to make this an evening of enchantment for her, even if he had to endure a night of screeching opera singers and matchmaking mothers.

But there would also be an orchestra and dancing afterward.

Did Abby know how to dance?

He didn't care.

He'd wait for a waltz to take her into his arms... all he had to do afterward was remember to let her go.

CHAPTER ELEVEN

ABBY'S LIP WAS still throbbing lightly as she entered Lady Miranda's home and was instantly enthralled by its elegance and festive decorations. Vases overflowing with freshly cut flowers surrounded the entry hall. Scented candles blazed in gleaming, silver candelabra and chandeliers. Elegantly dressed ladies and gentlemen were milling about with champagne flutes in hand and smiles on their faces.

Music and laughter filled the air, as did the heavenly aroma of nutmeg, cinnamon, and plum juices that wafted in from the dining room.

Tynan grinned. "Impressed?"

"Very." She tried her best not to look like a poor country cousin visiting London for the very first time, but could not help gaping at the splendor and gaiety. She glanced down at her attire, hoping the simple gown of ecru silk trimmed with ecru lace was not too badly out of fashion. It was two years old and had never been worn until now for lack of an occasion. There were no pearl beads or satin ribbons and bows to adorn the delicate fabric. Her only jewelry was a pair of teardrop pearl earrings that would hardly be noticed for the wisps of curls that framed her face.

Tynan must have realized what she was thinking. "Fretting about your appearance?"

She nodded.

"Don't. You're the prettiest girl here."

She laughed. "We haven't entered the music room yet. You haven't seen anyone but me so far."

His expression turned achingly tender. "I don't need to. I know a diamond when I see one."

There was something wonderful about the soft, seductive rumble of his voice that made her blush to her roots. No one had ever paid her such a compliment before. Indeed, no one had ever paid attention to her before.

She had no chance to respond to Tynan's comment before his brothers noticed them and bounded toward them like excited pups. Although one could hardly consider them pups, for they were big and broad shouldered, and brawny as gladiators. Abby's heart swelled with joy to see how much Tynan's brothers loved him. But they were brothers, so instead of simply greeting him, they punched his arm. They called him an arse and berated him for being late.

But to Abby's relief, they behaved like perfect gentlemen toward her, greeting her with a cordial warmth that brought a smile to her face and stuck it on permanently. "Miss Croft, a pleasure to see you again," Ronan said, his emerald green eyes as dark and brilliant as Tynan's. This handsome, young man would be a heartbreaker, she had no doubt. "I'm glad my brother had the good sense to bring you. My mother will be delighted, as are we all."

Joshua called over one of the footmen and lifted a glass of champagne off his tray. "For you, Abigail."

"What about me?" Tynan griped.

"Get it yourself," Finn said with a laugh, turning to Abby and holding out his arm. "May I escort you to my mother and then to supper?"

"No, you may not," Tynan muttered. "Abby is with me. I'll escort her to Mother. I'll take her in to supper. You are not to go near her. None of you."

They blithely ignored him.

Ronan merely shrugged. "Miss Croft, there will be dancing after the opera singer has finished assaulting our eardrums. May I claim a dance?"

"Me too," his other two brothers said at the same time.

Abby hadn't thought about that. "I'm so sorry. I would love to, but I can't. You see, I never learned how to dance." She tried not let her dismay show, but she was terrible at hiding her feelings, so they all noticed immediately. "But thank you so much for asking me. I... there's so much I don't know... perhaps it wasn't a good idea to–"

"Abby," Tynan said softly, "you belong with us. You'll do just fine. These clods can't dance either. They would have destroyed your feet."

Ronan nodded. "We're glad you're here. Don't hesitate to turn to us for help. If anyone is rude to you or gives you a difficult time, let us know. We'll take care of it."

Finn and Joshua crossed their massive arms over their chests and nodded.

Abby's insides melted. She liked having these gladiator bodyguards to protect her. She liked having people around her who cared if she were dead or alive. Indeed, she'd felt quite dead inside lately.

"Come along, Abby. Mother's just spotted us." Tynan took her arm in his once more. "We'd better go to her before she tramples anyone who has the misfortune to be caught standing between us."

Tynan's mother welcomed her like a daughter and, after shooing her son away, began to introduce her to her guests. "This delightful young lady is Miss Abigail Croft. She and the Countess of Exmoor are inseparable companions," Lady Miranda said, conveniently neglecting to mention that she'd only met Sophie and James twice and hadn't met a single Brayden until this week. "She is also one of my dearest friends."

"Westcliff seems quite taken with you," a friend of Miranda's, Lady Hester, said quite kindly, her tone gentle and not at all snide. "He's been seen escorting you about town. And he hasn't taken his eyes off you ever since Lady Miranda snatched you away from him"

Abby didn't quite know how to respond. "He's been helping my brother."

"Indeed," Miranda said with a sad shake of her head, "her brother is quite ill and we've all been pitching in to help. Lord Coventry, too."

Lady Hester's eyebrows shot up in surprise. "Ah, my dear. I had no idea you were connected to Lord Coventry as well."

Miranda spoke for her before she had the time to formulate a response. "Coventry is like a father to Abigail and her brother."

Abby tried not to roll her eyes. This was taking matters a bit too far. "Lord Coventry has generously opened his home in Falmouth to us. You see, we hope the sea air will restore my–"

Lady Hester's eye lit up. "Does Lady Withnall know?"

Abby regarded her in confusion. "Who is Lady Withnall?"

"Only the biggest gossip in London," Tynan said, returning to her side at the same time Lady Hester mumbled a hasty excuse to take her leave and sprinted off toward a small crowd of women standing in a corner. "And Lady Hester will now run to her with the juicy information. It's quite a coup, for Lady Withnall is usually the first to learn of anything. She has the ears of a bat and the eyes of a hawk."

Abby could not help but grin. "Is she here?"

He nodded. "And she's been quietly circling around you ever since you walked in on my arm. She's the little harridan holding court in the corner, the one with the walking cane in hand. Be nice to her or she might club you over the head with it."

His mother frowned at him, although she did not seem very angry. "Honestly, Westcliff. Is that any way to speak of my guests?"

He cast Lady Miranda an innocent look. "Your opera singer is about to start yowling and I promised to escort Abigail in. We want to claim the best seats, of course."

He took Abby's arm in his and led her away before his mother had a chance to comment on his blatant lie. He'd made no secret of his dislike of these musicales. The concert room was already filling with guests eager to hear the dulcet operatic tones, but Abby could feel the tension building within Tynan, and was surprised when he took the seat beside her. "You're staying?"

He winced. "Yes. I'm not letting you out of my sight."

She shook her head and laughed. "I'm quite safe here. Please don't feel you must stay by my side all evening."

He regarded her intently. "You're the only reason I'm here. And you're not in the least safe. There are easily a dozen men who intend to approach you the moment my back is turned. You're the prettiest girl here, as I've told you. And I'm not letting any of them come near you."

"Why not?" She wasn't seeking compliments from him, but merely asking a question. He'd made it abundantly clear that he was quite content with his state of bachelorhood and had no intention of making any changes.

"The music's starting," he grumbled, shooting her a hot, possessive glance.

Was it possible he was thinking of making changes? Should she dare hope that he might consider courting her? It was safest not to make too much of his actions. But she found his attentiveness most confusing. He sat beside her throughout the recital and then escorted her to supper, sitting beside her while she delighted in the carved meats set out at one end and the sweets set out at the other end of the enormous dining table. "Are you enjoying the evening, Abby?"

She swallowed her bite of lemon cake and nodded. "Very much. It's been magical."

His lips curved into a smile. "Good. There's more fun in store." He rose and held out his hand to her.

She set down her cake and brushed the crumbs off her fingers before taking his offered hand. But she froze when they stepped into the ballroom and she realized his purpose. The music room had been small and intimate, but the ballroom was large and grand and filled with guests enjoying the steps of a quadrille. "I don't know how to dance, remember?"

"I remember." He walked her around the edge of the room until they'd reached the double doors that led onto the balcony. "The waltz is next.

We'll dance out here, where no one will notice you. Just trust me, Abby. Follow my lead and let me guide you. You'll do fine."

He was wrong about no one noticing them. Although everyone was busy dancing, they were concentrating their attention on her and Tynan, not on the steps they had easily mastered throughout their years of training to make their way in Society.

She'd had no such training.

But the notion of sharing a waltz with Tynan under the moonlight was too tempting to pass up. The quadrille was just ending by the time they walked onto the balcony. They were the only ones outdoors. She wasn't certain whether it was mere coincidence or by purposeful design. Had he engaged his brothers to block everyone else's access out here? She would not have been surprised, for these Braydens were quite loyal to each other, and were definitely plotting to make this evening perfect for her.

Obviously, this was Tynan's doing. She was glad he was being incredibly nice to her, but it was a bit much. Everyone would think he was besotted with her. She supposed it didn't matter, for they'd learn the truth soon enough. He meant well, so she resolved to stop questioning his motives and simply enjoy what remained of the evening.

The big, silver moon and brilliant stars were shining in the night sky. If there was a bite to the crisp October air, she didn't feel it. Indeed, she felt nothing but warmth and excitement as the strains of the melodic waltz filled the air and Tynan drew her into his arms. "Put your hand in mine, Abby."

His voice was low and husky.

When she hesitated, he simply took it in his. "When I step forward, you'll take a matching step back. Just follow me when I turn. We'll take it slow."

There were a hundred friends and family inside, all of whom were now openly staring at them. However, Abby felt as though she and Tynan were alone in a beautiful dream. She never wanted this moment to end. She loved the heat of his big, rough hand at the small of her back. She loved the sandalwood scent of him. She melted at his soft smile and the wickedly tender gleam in his eyes.

I don't ever want to wake up from this dream.

She meant to look at her feet, but Tynan's gaze was entrancing and she could not look away. Oh, this had to be make believe. She could not possibly be dancing under the moonlight with the handsomest bachelor in England. "Abby, your eyes are watering."

"I know. I'm about to cry, but this time for joy. You're doing this on purpose, aren't you? Giving me a magical memory."

He twirled her as the waltz continued. "Are you angry?"

"No. I'll treasure this evening. I know how difficult these next few months will be with Peter. I'll fall into bed each night and dream of you holding me in your arms and this beautiful music filling the air."

She sighed before continuing. "But I have a request to make of you."

"Anything, Abby."

She nodded. "Stop. Please, stop. I know you mean well, but I'm more than halfway in love with you. I don't have the strength to resist you. So, if you can never love me, then put an end to this beautiful pretense and take me home now."

He looked pained, for she'd obviously caught him by surprise.

She must have sounded ungrateful. She didn't mean to, but he roused such alarmingly deep feelings in her. "My heart is happiest when I'm with you, Tynan. You make my every moment with you feel magical. I forget what is real. I hardly know you, and yet it seems like I've known you all of my life. Perhaps I've been waiting for you all of my life and never realized it. I don't know how else to express what I'm feeling. Oh, dear. You're frowning. I've ruined your plans, haven't I? I've said too much."

He was indeed frowning and looked unsettled, perhaps angry.

She sighed. "But you must understand. I've never fallen in love before. It quite overwhelms me. In truth, it scares the wits out of me."

"Abby..." Her name came out in an aching groan.

She sighed. "Now I sound completely unappreciative and it wasn't my intent at all. Forget I said anything. It's an enchanted night and you will always be my perfect knight in shining armor. My heart will get over you."

His silence was like a heavy, unsettling fog that swirled between them.

She cleared her throat. "Will you excuse me?"

He released her, or perhaps she was the one who'd skittered away. He made no move to follow her indoors when she fled from the balcony.

She headed for the ladies' retiring room, knowing he could not follow her in there. But she did not find the peace she'd sought, for seated on the divan were two women of obvious sophistication and elegance. They cast her a disdainful glance and then promptly ignored her. Or perhaps they knew exactly who she was and were determined to cut her to ribbons. "Will you be seeing Westcliff this evening?" one of the fine ladies asked the other.

At first, Abby thought they were addressing her, but quickly realized the conversation was exclusive to the pair and spoken aloud for her benefit.

"Yes," said the other one, an elegant beauty with dark hair and striking, pale green eyes. "My husband's out of town, and Westcliff must first get rid of the little nuisance he's been stuck escorting around London this week. But he's pent up and randy. The sex will be hot and intense between us."

"Isn't it always with him?" the first one remarked. "He enjoys his bed games."

Abby couldn't breathe.

The ladies got up and walked past her as though she did not exist.

She'd almost believed Tynan had taken a fancy to her, but these ladies had made sure to put her in her place. He was merely being polite, treating her as his pet project. He didn't love her and was likely trying to figure out how to distance himself from her right now. She'd told him that she loved him... almost. She'd held back the littlest bit, but he had to know her feelings for him. She wasn't merely on her way to falling in love with him. She was there already. Deeply and unabashedly in love with this man who was more perfect than anyone she could ever have conjured up in a dream.

No wonder he'd kept silent as she'd prattled. He was horrified.

She left the ladies' retiring room and was about to make her way downstairs when she saw this same woman who'd been bragging about her exploits with Tynan now talking to a gentleman. She closed her eyes and swallowed hard. Don't let it be Tynan.

Of course, it was.

"Lady Bascom," he said, giving her a curt bow.

She wasted no time in putting her hands all over him. "Lord Bascom is out of town. I'll see you tonight at the club. We'll catch up where we left off."

The peacock feather.

The black silk bindings.

The strawberries... those were quite delicious... and meant for Lady Bascom.

"I'm busy tonight," Tynan surprised her by responding. "We'll catch up another time."

The beauty did not seem pleased and left in a snit.

Tynan raked a hand through his hair and chose that moment to turn his gaze to the stairs. "Abby. Hell, did you hear that exchange? It isn't what you think."

"Please take me home, Lord Westcliff. I've suddenly developed a terrible headache." Because it was exactly what she'd thought. He enjoyed 'sophisticated' woman, and she was a naive virgin who'd just embarrassed him by admitting that she loved him. "Better yet, perhaps Lord and Lady Exmoor can drop me off on their way home. You needn't trouble yourself with me any longer."

Tynan grabbed her arm.

His expression was thunderous. "I'll take you home. I'm not trusting you to anyone else. You're my responsibility." He paused and muttered under his breath. "You're not a responsibility, you're a pleasure."

"Hah!" If that wasn't an outright lie, she didn't know what was.

His eyes were a dark and turbulent, fiery green. "You're no trouble to me, Abby. You never have been and never will be. Got that?"

"No, I don't 'get' any of this. Just take me home before we create a scene. I can't wait for this night to end."

"Bollocks." But he called for his carriage and they were soon in it, making their way back to her townhouse.

Abby didn't think this night could get any worse.

She was trapped in this carriage with the man she loved and who didn't love her back. Not only did he not love her, he was merely biding his time until he could be rid of her. Indeed, this night could not get any worse.

But she was wrong.

When the carriage rolled to a stop, she climbed down on her own and strode to her front door. It was wide open and unattended. Oh, no. What now? Jameson and Sally hurried down the hall stairs as she walked in. "Miss Abigail, he knocked Vickers out with a candlestick and escaped."

"Peter?" She thought her brother was too weak to lift himself out of bed, much less best his beefy valet.

Jameson nodded. "We're so sorry, Miss Abigail. We should have been watching him closer. A friend of his paid a call, but he was with Lord Peter for no more than five minutes before he left. He appeared quite respectable. An old school mate of his lordship's, he claimed to be. This is all my fault."

Abby's insides were now twisted into Gordian knots. "No, he's tricked us all." She marched into the study and withdrew a pair of pistols. "But I know where he's going and I–"

"Give me those." Tynan crossed the room in two strides and came up behind her to grab the pistols out of her hands. "You're not going anywhere. I'll go."

"You?" She frowned at him, wishing she still had the pistols to use on him. "I don't need your assistance. I know how much of an imposition I've been on you. He's my brother. I'll take care of it."

He held the pistols out of her reach. "You will not. I'll take care of it. You're to stay here, safe and out of trouble. I'll tie you up and lock you in your wardrobe if I have to."

"Why? I'm absolving you of any duty you have toward me or my brother. Go away. Go play your lurid games with those tawdry beauties. Just leave me alone."

"I can't, damn it." He set down the pistols and hauled her over his shoulder.

"What are you doing? Put me down!"

He strode into the entry hall where Sally and Jameson were staring wide eyed at him and the sight of her derriere on prominent display over his shoulder. "I need rope and a latchkey."

Abby gasped. "I forbid you to obey him!"

Jameson ignored her. Sally shook her head and sighed. "He only means to protect you, Miss Abigail. You'll be killed if you go after your brother."

In her heart, she knew Sally was right. Worse, she knew that Tynan meant to risk his own life to save Peter. She struggled harder as he climbed the stairs with steadfast determination, then realized she was going about it all wrong and stopped struggling. By this time, he'd reached her bedchamber door. "Put me down, Tynan," she said in a ragged plea, tugging lightly on his hair. "Neither of us will go. I can't do this anymore."

He opened the door and strode in as though he had every right to be in here with her.

"Tynan, listen to me."

He shut the door behind him, closing them both in her chamber. She did not bother to point out the inappropriateness of his conduct. He was quite aware, but too angry to care. She sighed. "There's no need to hold me against my will. I won't risk my life to save him when he has no wish to be saved, and I certainly won't allow you to risk your life. He'll find his way home tomorrow morning. We'll let Dr. Farthingale know what happened and ask him to start the treatments all over again."

His own anger appeared to abate as he eased her off his shoulder. She slid down the hard length of him, trying desperately to quell her tingles as he gently set her down. His gaze was exquisitely tender, no sign of frustration or anger. Of course, he hadn't really been angry with her, just this seemingly hopeless situation. "I'm so sorry, Abby."

"I know." She released a shuddering breath, sad that all her good intentions toward her brother had been for naught. But also sad because Tynan was still standing close and she loved him more than ever. She was still tingling and aching to be in his arms. "I owe you an apology for more than this episode with the pistols."

He cupped her cheek in his warm hand. "No, Abby. You don't. You have every right to be overset."

"But I treated you unfairly at your mother's musicale. You didn't do anything wrong. If anything, it was too right. You made me feel so special and loved... I simply didn't know how to handle it. I know you don't love me. I know you enjoy your freedom. But I'm no less in love with you because of it. You've been nothing but generous with me. I only wish our waltz on the balcony had meant as much to you as it had to me."

She turned away from him because it hurt too much to know this wonderful man was going to walk out the door and she might never see him again. "Good night, Tynan. Enjoy the rest of your evening."

She did not look back when she heard his retreating footsteps and then the creak of her door as he opened it and then softly shut it behind him.

It wasn't a pretty ending to their time together, but it was better this way. Tomorrow would have been their last day together, so it mattered little if he did not come around in the morning. In truth, it was easier this way. A quick, abrupt end. She'd pack on her own tomorrow. *I love you, Tynan. Enjoy the rest of your life.*

CHAPTER TWELVE

SINCE TYNAN HAD employed Bow Street runners to watch Peter's movements, he knew Abby's brother could not have slipped away unnoticed. The only question was whether his runners had stopped him on the street and were bringing him home now or were following him to his ultimate destination.

It mattered little, for Tynan knew where Peter was going.

Tynan had just turned the corner from the Whitpool townhouse when he spotted one of his Bow Street runners, Homer Barrow, hurrying toward him. "M'lord, I was just about to go in search of you. My associate, Mick, is following Lord Whitpool. A friend of his lordship's came round earlier to pay him a visit. They must have planned his escape in the few minutes his friend was there, for there was a carriage standing right here on the corner, no doubt in wait for him, and he jumped in it."

"Thank you, Mr. Barrow." He glanced toward his own carriage still in front of Abby's house. "Come with me. We'll try to cut them off before they reach Bedford Place."

The man's jowls wobbled as he shook his head. "And what will we do if he's gone into that establishment already?"

Tynan ran a hand roughly through his hair. "I'll gather some of the earls. Sunderland, Harrington, Sussex, Wainthorpe–"

"No, m'lord. I've no doubt you know how to handle yourself in a fight, but let me and Mick handle it. Bribery is just as effective and no blood shall be spilled. We'll get him out quietly. All I ask is that you loan us your carriage to bring him home once we've accomplished the task."

The desire to break into that opium den and tear it apart was strong. The desire to tear Peter apart, limb from limb, was even stronger, for he'd hurt Abby so badly. But reason won out. "Very well, Mr. Barrow. I'll gather the earls and have them at the ready on the chance you encounter a problem. We aren't afraid of a fight."

He climbed into his carriage, motioned for the Bow Street runner to climb in after him, and then instructed his coachman to make all speed to the Wicked Earls' Club. As the carriage clattered down the familiar streets, he and Homer went over their plan.

The purpose was to remove Abby's brother with minimal attention. No fights, although Tynan half hoped there would be one. He was angry and frustrated, and did not care how flimsy his excuse was to disrupt whatever went on in there. Coventry had quietly approached his royal connections and insisted something be done about this casual use of opium long ago. But neither the royal family nor the Privy Council considered it important enough to merit their immediate attention. Too many people still considered it a fashionable amusement, a way to expand one's mind and creative talents.

Peter was not uniquely affected by the dark side of this elegant indulgence. Spasms, convulsions, and worse were common among this fast crowd.

Tynan rubbed his hands over his face and groaned. "This is a bloody mess."

He still itched for a fight, but knew better than to start one. He and his fellow earls could have gone in and extracted Abby's brother with little resistance, but to do so would put all of them at risk. The artists and poets were not dangerous, but their opium suppliers were. These scoundrels were not the sort to follow rules of engagement. They'd wait to catch him or any of the other earls by surprise, stick a knife between their ribs, and leave them to bleed out upon the cobblestones.

He reached into his coat pocket as the carriage turned onto Bedford Place. "How much blunt do you need?"

Bribery was the safest way to go. Still, he made quick work of gathering the few earls present at the club. Wainthorpe was never one to back down from a battle. He even had a dark and dangerous look about him. Sunderland was just as eager to help. Perhaps they'd all grown restless and were looking for something more out of life. He could only speak for himself, but these hollow, nightly pleasures were growing quite dull.

While Homer and Mick spoke to the guards at the neighbor's door, Tynan waited in the shadows, standing close enough to hear either of the runners call out for help if something went wrong. The other earls stood not far behind, and Tynan could sense everyone's tension in the thick, misty air. The wind was blowing off the Thames. The scent of fish and bilge water carried on the intermittent gusts.

Within moments, Homer and Mick returned carrying Abby's brother between them. "They wanted him out of there as badly as we did, m'lord. Handed him to us before I'd reached into m'pocket to offer them a bribe. A dead body ain't good for business, you see. And Miss Croft's brother is as close to dead as a man can be and still be breathing."

"I'll have my carriage brought around to take him home."

"Beggin' your pardon, m'lord. He ain't in no shape to be sent home," Mick said. "Is there somewhere we can set him down in the club? He's a filthy mess. Been casting up his accounts, heaving so hard, there's nothin' left to come up but his own blood."

Tynan nodded. "There's a small room off the kitchen. Settle him in there for now. I'll send in two of the maids to clean him up."

Wainthorpe, who had come to stand beside him the moment the runners came out of the house, cast him a concerned glance. "I'll have one of the footmen summon a doctor."

Tynan nodded. "Dr. Farthingale's been treating him."

"What's to be done about Miss Croft?" Homer asked. "Shall I let her know that her brother will remain here for the night?"

Tynan nodded again. "Yes, at once. She'll be awake and worriedly pacing. I'll stay with her brother until the doctor arrives. Tell her that I'll bring her brother home in the morning." He didn't bother to add what all of them were thinking, that he'd likely be bringing her brother home in a wooden box.

He glanced around as the other earls came forward, their expressions equally grim. "Hell," Tynan said quietly, "Mr. Barrow, you'd better bring Miss Croft here. I'll sit with her brother until she arrives."

He wanted so badly to be the one to go to Abby and tell her what happened. He knew she'd be devastated and in need of support. He wanted to be the one to take her in his arms and assure her that she would not be alone through this ordeal. But he dared not leave her brother just yet. If something were to happen to the worthless bounder, he knew it would be easier for Abby to endure her grief knowing that someone was by her brother's side to the very end.

Perhaps it was foolish on his part to think so, but in his heart, he truly believed it would help her come to terms with his... he did not wish to think it.

Once Abby's brother was cleaned up and settled, and the Bow Street runners had gone off to report to Abby, Tynan grabbed a chair and sat by his side to await Dr. Farthingale. It wasn't long before Abby's brother was moaning and restlessly turning from side to side. "Where am I? What are you doing here?"

Tynan shifted forward, his body aching slightly from sitting in the small, uncomfortable chair. Was Peter delirious or actually talking to him? "You abandoned Abby, you bastard. When are you going to think of her instead of yourself?"

Not the words of kindness and healing that Abby would have spoken, but Tynan was too angry to care.

Peter's eyes drifted open. "Abby?" He began to cry. "Abby, I'm so sorry. I'm so sorry, my dearest. I love you, Abby. Forgive me. I never meant to fail you."

Tynan curled his hands into fists, wanting to pummel her brother even as his heart ached. He wanted so badly to give Abby back her happy family. She deserved better than the life she had been given.

Her brother continued to ramble in his delirium. "Abby, you're the strong one. You always have been. You're my rock. My anchor. I love you."

Tynan rose and began to pace across the tiny room, suddenly feeling as though the walls were closing in on him. The space was about the size of a butler's pantry and primarily used to store overflow supplies, for Coventry held grand parties at the club every once in a while... nothing respectable. These were nights of bacchanal. No spouses were ever invited.

Yet Coventry never participated.

He and Lady Coventry were a love match.

So why had he formed this Wicked Earls' Club and invited a select few earls to join? All bachelors, and all... perhaps all were as restless and off course as he was. Perhaps he wasn't the only one needing something more in his life and not knowing where to find it.

There was no window in the room, but there were two doors. One led into the kitchen and the other opened onto the back of the house. Both doors were closed at the moment. Tynan was finding it hard to breathe in the confined space. Since Peter was well enough tucked under his covers to manage a bit of cool air, Tynan opened the door and stepped outside a moment.

He breathed in the cold, damp air.

The scent of impending rain penetrated his nostrils and turned his skin clammy.

He glanced up. The clouds had thickened considerably, obliterating the silver moon and any hint of stars. He'd been standing outdoors for less than a minute before he heard a slight commotion by the kitchen door.

His heart began to beat like thunder in his chest.

Abby had arrived.

He stepped back inside to greet her and tell her all that had happened, but she ran into his arms before he managed a word and hugged him with all her might. Wordlessly, he wrapped his arms around her trembling body and held her tightly. He felt the strong the beat of her heart against his chest, the beats as rapid as those of a frightened rabbit.

That's what she was, his little rabbit.

Soft, gentle, and defenseless from those who would hunt and destroy her.

"You stayed with him," she said in a shattered whisper, recognizing what he'd done. "Thank you."

It hadn't been a foolish thought to remain by his side, after all. "I did it for you, Abby."

In truth, the notion that he would do anything and everything for this girl seemed so natural and right. The intensity of his feelings caught him by surprise. But he would not deny them. He'd jump into the Thames if she asked him to. He'd walk through fire to save her.

He'd protect her forever.

"Abby. Abby, my dearest. Is that you?" Peter was calling to her, so she slipped out of Tynan's arms and hurried to her brother's side. *The undeserving bastard.* "I'm so sorry. I love you."

Tynan's hands curled into fists. He couldn't help it. If the bounder had ever spared a thought for his sister, he wouldn't have put her through this punishment. He would have understood his duty to her and fought to heal himself. He was capable of it. The man wasn't a coward. He'd commanded a regiment and acquitted himself bravely. So where had all that courage fled?

Dr. Farthingale arrived as Peter was about to spout more hollow words of affection to Abby, sparing them all from having to listen to him. Abby flinched every time her brother said 'I love you' to her, as though her brother had slapped her instead of provided comfort.

"Sorry to disrupt your evening, Dr. Farthingale," Abby said, her voice strained and her gaze despairing. "But I'm glad you're here."

The doctor's expression was unmistakably grim. "Miss Croft, you look all done in. Why don't you allow Lord Westcliff to take you into the kitchen for a cup of tea? I'll call you once I've finished examining your brother."

She resisted. "I'm not thirsty. I had better stay. I want to be here if..."

She squared her shoulders and tipped her chin up. "If he takes his last breath."

The doctor gave a curt nod. "Very well."

Tynan drew Abby up against him so that her back was leaning against his chest. He wrapped his arms around her, relieved when she nestled in them without protest and rested her head on his shoulder. Her hands were cold so he covered them with his and rubbed his thumbs along the tips of her fingers to warm them.

She nuzzled his shoulder, silently conveying her gratitude.

He tried not to think how perfectly she fit against him, how perfectly their bodies seemed to cleave to one another. Everything about Abby seemed to fit him right. Her sweetness that was a perfect counter to his aloofness. Her quiet strength that was a match for his arrogance. Her innocence that was more potent than the sexual arts practiced by the sophisticated courtesans of his acquaintance.

Abby's tension seemed to ease at his touch, but her attention was not on him. It remained fixed on her brother, and the bounder was putting her through every high and low imaginable. Tynan's arms stayed firmly around her, even as she watched in horror as her brother coughed up blood and then fell into convulsions.

"Tynan, I can't bear it."

He turned her in his arms so that she now faced him. "Let me take you into the kitchen."

"No, I need to be here." But she closed her eyes and rested her cheek against his chest. Her hands gripped his shoulders so tightly, and he knew that what she really wanted to do was put her hands to her ears to muffle her brother's cries.

"I have you, Abby. I won't let go of you." Tynan was certain this was the end, but after a few agonizingly tense moments, Dr. Farthingale managed to bring Abby's brother back. As he revived, he once again began to spout 'I love you' to Abby, his words merely serving to tear her heart to shreds.

Tynan could no longer bear to watch Abby suffer over the fading shadow that was her brother. "He's in the doctor's care. You need to take care of yourself now." He scooped her into his arms and carried her up the back stairs of the club to his private chamber.

Tynan had expected her to protest, but she circled her arms around his neck instead and cried silent tears.

He opened the door to his chamber and settled her on the bed. He wanted her to lie down and try to get some rest, for she'd been up all night. So had he, but he was too angry to sleep. Besides, he couldn't very well fall into bed with her, much as he would have wanted to under other circumstances. "Close your eyes for an hour," he said, bending on one knee to remove her shoes. "I'll wake you if something happens sooner."

Her eyes were glistening with unshed tears. "I thought I'd get here and he'd be dead."

"I know, sweetheart." He'd often used endearments with other women, especially when taking them to his bed, but this was so different. He meant it with Abby. She was his sweetheart. And he was going to protect her.

He'd vowed to Coventry that he'd marry her if he took her innocence.

He hadn't taken it yet.

It wasn't from lack of wanting to.

She was the only woman he wanted now.

He knew by the look in her eyes that he could have her without benefit of marriage. He didn't have to propose to her. *Bollocks.* But he was going to. He wanted to marry Abby and it was important that she and Coventry and his entire family understand that he was offering to make her his wife because he wanted her, not because he was fulfilling the oath he'd given Coventry.

He was already on his knees. All he had to do was say the words. "Abby, I—"

A footman pounded on his open door, startling both of them. "Lord Westcliff, the doctor says to come right away!"

CHAPTER THIRTEEN

ABBY LEAPED OFF Tynan's bed and raced downstairs, not caring that she was in her stockinged feet and could feel the prickle of cold stone against her heels as she crossed from the kitchen into the storage room where her brother lay dying.

Tynan was by her side, steadfastly determined to protect her from whatever was about to befall her. She loved this wonderful man, this wickedly handsome earl. She loved him so deeply. That he'd remained by her side throughout this turbulent week was a miracle. She didn't quite understand why he was doing all this for her. Perhaps he felt some misguided affection for her as well. He certainly couldn't love her. Not even a saint would have stuck by her side throughout this unrelentingly miserable ordeal. "Dr. Farthingale, what's happened?"

At first, she couldn't seem to breathe.

Then her breaths came so fast, she couldn't seem to stop them until Tynan put a gentle hand on her shoulder, silently assuring her that she was not alone. She gave him a small nod of acknowledgment as she regained control of herself. Would he help her with the funeral arrangements? Would he stay by her side until her brother's body was buried beside those of her parents and her brothers... she'd lost two of them at sea and their bodies had never been recovered.

Another unfinished Croft family matter.

"I didn't mean to startle you by summoning you here," the doctor said, bringing her thoughts back to the present. "Your brother is resting and stable. But he isn't strong enough yet to make the trip to Falmouth. It must be postponed another week, perhaps two." He rose and approached her. "I don't know if this is a turning point for him. He's fallen low enough into the slime that even he is repulsed by his behavior."

Abby did not dare to get her hopes up. She'd been through

disappointment too often to believe a word of what her brother said. "He's sworn as much to me before. Then the craving strikes and he becomes a rabid beast."

Dr. Farthingale regarded her sympathetically. "I know. It won't be easy. But there's a look in his eyes that I haven't seen before. Shame. Regret. Whatever it is, I hope this will mark the first step in his long road to recovery." He then turned to Tynan in expectation.

Abby wondered what the doctor wanted of Tynan. To remain by her side throughout Peter's treatment? She still didn't understand why he was by her side now, doing all of this for her.

Tynan squeezed her shoulder once again for reassurance. "I'll provide whatever Miss Croft needs, Dr. Farthingale. Just tell us what to do and I'll arrange it."

"Thank you, Lord Westcliff." He resumed his seat beside Peter. "I'll watch him for the next few hours. As for the two of you, it's obvious you've been up all night dealing with the mess Miss Croft's brother created. Get some rest, Miss Croft. You'll need all your strength and wits about you when dealing with your brother."

"Doctor, please tell me the truth," she said, her words breathless and shattered. "What are the chances of his ever regaining his health?"

He hesitated a long moment. "Slim, but not hopeless."

But his hesitation said it all. It was hopeless. Dr. Farthingale simply didn't have the heart to tell her so. "Thank you."

She turned and slowly walked through the kitchen, up the back stairs to Tynan's bedchamber. Tynan followed a few steps behind, giving her enough space so that he was not hovering over her, but still keeping her in his sight. Was he that worried about her? Did he think she would do something foolish?

Her mind was surprisingly clear.

She knew what she had to do next.

She walked into Tynan's room and sat on his bed.

He followed her in and closed the door. Not only closed it, but latched it to keep everyone else out. Good. It saved her the bother of doing it herself. "Abby, we have to talk."

She shook her head and laughed. "Oh, no. I'm through talking. I'm through worrying about others. I'm through sacrificing for others and getting kicked in the teeth for it." She unrolled her stockings and tossed them over the footboard.

Tynan hadn't noticed because he'd turned his back to her in order to add another log onto the dwindling fire. His eyes rounded in surprise when he turned to face her again and noticed that her legs were bare. "Are your stockings wet?" He scooped them off the footboard and put them to hang over the mantel, using pegs to hold them in place while they dried by the heat of the flames.

She began to fumble with the buttons of her gown.

Tynan groaned. "What are you doing?"

"Isn't it obvious? I'm undressing. Shouldn't one be undressed when one is setting about to lose one's virginity?" Her hands were shaking. "Wretched buttons. Whoever invented these instruments of torture?"

Tynan was by her side in two strides, his hands over hers. "Stop, Abby. You don't know what you're saying."

She met his gaze, and melted at the tenderness reflected in his beautiful green eyes. "I'm a woman of no means, about to lose the last of my family. You saw the doctor's hesitation. There is no chance that Peter will heal. I will soon be alone in the world for the rest of my life. But I am also sitting here with the handsomest, wicked earl in England. So, if you think I'm going to pass up the opportunity for an unforgettable night of pleasure in your arms... well, it will be daytime soon. But, no matter. The point is, I would like to be loved by you. I would like to feel the warmth of your skin against my palms. I would like to feel the heat of your kisses on my lips and anywhere else you deem appropriate on my body."

She was making a fool of herself.

He was looking at her aghast.

She didn't care. "I won't expect anything of you in return, of course."

He arched an eyebrow. "I see. You only want me as your stud bull."

Why was he being so difficult? "You know that you mean far more to me than that. I'd never give myself to anyone but you. Indeed, you mean everything to me. But the fact that I love you is my problem not yours. It doesn't mean you owe me anything."

She resumed fumbling with her buttons. "But I do have one request of you."

He groaned lightly. "What is it?"

She cleared her throat and heat rose in her cheeks because she knew her request was highly improper. But everything she was doing now was improper, so why not add one more sin to the pile? "Before I leave this room... before you finish, you know..."

"Having my way with you?"

She cleared her throat again and nodded. "I'd like to find out what is so special about that peacock feather."

He laughed heartily as he bent on one knee and began to fasten the buttons she'd just undone. She placed her hands on his to stop him, but he wasn't taking the hint. "What are you doing? I'm trying to shed my clothes to give you unimpeded access to my body. It would please me immensely if you did the same with yours."

He was still laughing. "No."

"What?" She blinked her eyes.

"I said, no."

His laughter faded and he now looked quite earnest. Impossibly serious. *Oh, dear.* What had she just done? "Oh, I see. You don't want me." It hadn't occurred to her. But why should he want her when she paled in comparison to Society's Incomparables?

"Not like this. I don't want you like this."

Her heart sank into her toes. "Of course, I should have known that I'm meager fare compared to... I understand that you're not interested in me. Why would you want me after all I've put you through? I'm so sorry. I didn't mean to impose myself on you. I just thought... you're notorious... you take any woman into your bed, and I–"

He confused her by stopping her mouth with a deep and gentle kiss that wrapped itself around her heart and wouldn't let go. She melted into a liquid pool of delight and was still melting by the time he ended the kiss. "I want you in my bed, Abby. Not just for one night."

"You do?" She glanced out the window. "It's almost daylight."

His grin returned and it was appealingly wicked. "You're missing my obvious point."

"And that is?" Her eyes suddenly rounded in surprise. "You wish to make me your mistress?"

"Bollocks, you're dense." He groaned. "Apparently, I'm not as obvious as I thought. Look at me, Abby. I am on bended knee beside you. What would that indicate?"

She didn't know. He was big, so he'd have to crouch down to be at her height in order to look her in the eyes. "My head's in a muddle. I'm still tingling from your kiss. I can't think at all. Help me out."

He caressed her cheek. "I made a vow to Coventry that if I took you to my bed, I'd marry you."

She gasped. "Oh, I am indeed dense! Is this the reason you won't show me a night of pleasure? He made you promise to marry me if you did."

"Quite so. But that's why I'm asking you now, before you remove a single stitch of clothing. Before I remove mine. Before I take you in my arms and plunder your beautiful body. I want you to know that I'm asking you of my own free will. I want you to know that I am under no compulsion to offer for you, so when I say the words, they will come straight from my heart."

"Words? From your heart?"

His grin remained enchantingly wicked. "Contrary to Society's opinion, I do have one."

She returned his smile with a glowing one of her own. "I know you do. It's the best heart I've ever encountered. It's the valiant heart of a gladiator. I love your heart."

"Well, that's promising."

"And I love you." She threw herself into his arms, almost toppling both of them.

"Abby!" He laughingly caught her and tightened his grasp to steady her. "This is what I love about you. You don't hold back. You give all of yourself." His expression turned tender. "And this wicked earl wants all of you." He paused to settle her on his lap and give her another heartfelt kiss. When he drew away, he was no longer grinning but remarkably serious once more. "Abby, my love. I want to share the rest of my life with you. Will you marry me?"

She was swallowed in his warm embrace, nestled against his magnificent body, her heart pounding so hard within her chest she could hardly breathe. Had she heard right? She pinched him.

He emitted a chuckle of surprise. "What did you do that for?"

Because he was a beautiful dream that had to come to an end. Isn't that what always happened? The moonlit enchantment inevitably faded with the first light of dawn. "I need to be certain you're real."

He pinched her very lightly on the forearm. "Did you feel that?"

She nodded.

"We're both real, Abby. I know this is all moving very fast for you. It is for me as well. In truth, I hardly know myself. But I do know that I love you."

"You do? I love you, too."

He smiled, obviously having more he wished to say to her. No doubt he believed more of an explanation was necessary. But it wasn't. He loved her and nothing else mattered. She was glad he still held her, for her heart was soaring so high, she might have floated upward to the raftered ceiling.

He kissed her on the nose before continuing. "I was lost the moment I saw you standing beside my window in the moon's soft glow. I had just rescued you and deposited you up here while trying to figure out what to do with you." He ran his thumb in a caress across her lips. "I've figured it out now. I want you beside me for always. That will not change, no matter what challenges we'll face going forward."

Her smile faltered. "Oh, Tynan. My brother, of course. How can I burden you with the mess he's created?"

He wrapped his arms more securely around her waist. "You're asking the wrong question, my love."

Her heart tugged at the husky lilt of his voice, and he'd called her *my love* as though he meant it. "What should I ask?"

"The right question is, how can I not stand beside the woman I love when she's so burdened? I know you would keep fighting for Peter all on your own. You've done an incredible job so far and no one could have done better. But you no longer have to fight alone. You have me. You have all of me. Now, will you answer my question?"

His lips were so close to hers, she did the only thing she could think of and kissed him fiercely. "Yes, my love. Yes, I will marry you, my wonderful Tynan. You're the noblest wicked earl I've ever met." She kissed him again, loving the warmth of his mouth on hers and the solid strength of his body as he drew her up against his muscled chest. "This is where I want to be. In the arms of the gladiator who saved me in more ways than one."

She waited for him to begin unfastening her buttons.

His gaze was hot and smoldering as he settled her on the bed and deftly removed her gown. He set it aside, but instead of removing her chemise next, he unpinned her hair and then tucked her under the covers. "Stay right there. Get some rest, for you shall have none when I return."

"When you return?" She drew the sheet up around her as she abruptly sat up. "Where are you going?"

He bent forward to kiss her possessively on the lips. "This is serious business, Abby. I need your brother's permission to marry you. I don't know who will have guardianship of you if... if he doesn't make it, so there's no time to waste. I also have to obtain the special license. Coventry will help me expedite it. Do you mind? Our wedding will be rushed."

She had no one but Peter left in the world. She had no pretensions about her situation. "Will your family be present for it?"

"Not if you don't want them." He winced. "Although I doubt I'll ever hear the end of it from my mother and aunts."

She laughed softly, her eyes agleam. "You mistake me meaning. I want them there. They're the closest thing to family I have. I can't wait to be able to claim them as my own. In truth, I wanted to hold on to them so tightly from the moment I met them."

She paused a moment, trying not to turn sloppily sentimental and weepy. "I prayed for them, Tynan... I prayed so hard that they would like me." She took a deep, ragged breath. "I was so tired of being alone. But despite my desperation, I knew that not just any family would do. I wanted a big, loving family. And then you introduced me to yours and they were perfect."

"Ah, don't tell them that." He cast her a boyish grin. "They'll never let me hear the end of it."

She couldn't help but laugh. "I've been given you *and* your family. I think you must pinch me again. This is more than a dream come true for me. This is a miracle, even more so because it isn't Christmas yet and everyone knows the best miracles happen then. We're only a few months off, so I suppose it counts. Yes, I want you. I want all of you."

"My family already loves you far better than they'll ever love me. They think I'm a debauched and arrogant ass."

She cupped his cheek in her palm, the bristles of his growth of beard prickling her skin. "No, you're my valiant earl. There's so much we still have to work out. There's Falmouth and Peter's recovery... assuming he..." She shook her head to dismiss those worries. "I'm so happy, Tynan. Do whatever you must... and one more thing."

He kissed the palm of her hand. "What is it, my love?"

"Don't forget the peacock feather."

CHAPTER FOURTEEN

TYNAN RETURNED THREE hours later to find Abby in a deep, contented sleep. She looked so beautiful with her dark hair splayed across his crisp, white pillows. She'd tossed the covers partially aside so that her slender legs were on full display, for her chemise had ridden up to her thighs. One of the sleeves of the chemise had fallen off her shoulder, displaying more creamy skin.

Mother in heaven.

The diaphanous fabric hid almost nothing.

He'd returned exhausted, but the sight of Abby in his bed sent a powerful jolt through him. He was wide awake now and ready to claim this beautiful girl with her brandy eyes and rose-tinged lips for his own. He didn't care that it was daylight and others would be stirring. The world around him seemed to disappear whenever he was with Abby.

He'd accomplished much in these few hours. He now had Peter's consent to the marriage and, thanks to Coventry, had the special license in his pocket. They could be married within the hour. But Abby wanted his family present. She'd asked so little of him, that he couldn't begrudge postponing the ceremony until tomorrow.

He'd worry about the betrothal contract later. Abby's brother was in no shape to negotiate it anyway. The terms mattered little, for he meant to protect Abby from this day forward, providing her a generous dower portion from his unentailed properties so that she'd never want for anything again.

He set down the bowl of strawberries he'd brought up for her on the chance she was awake and hungry, disappointed when she didn't stir from her sleep or so much as blink an eye. He came to her side and gently brushed a few stray curls off her cheek. Then, completely out of character for himself, he bent and kissed her brow before crossing the room and sinking onto the chair beside his desk to remove his boots.

Abby must have heard the light scrape of the chair against the wooden floor. She woke up with a start, but her smile when she saw him flooded the room with sunshine. "Tynan, I didn't hear you come in."

Her voice had a sultry depth to it as she shook off her haze of sleep.

She sat up and rubbed her eyes.

He stopped breathing when she arched her back and stretched like a contented kitten. Her chemise truly hid nothing of her body.

Mother in heaven.

He wanted to fling off his jacket, vest, and cravat. He wanted to rip off his shirt and claim this beautiful girl here and now. Where was the harm? They'd be married tomorrow. He got as far as taking off his jacket then stopped. Abby had just realized her state of undress and suddenly turned bashful. As she hastily wrapped the covers around herself, her gaze drifted to the strawberries.

Her eyes lit up. "Are those strawberries?"

He set his feet back in his boots and rose with a chuckle. "Yes, Abby. They're for you. I thought you might be hungry and I remembered how much you enjoyed them the first night we met."

She eased back and shook her head. "They were delicious. May I have them now?"

Her big, brandy eyes stared up at him with innocent anticipation.

Innocent.

That's what she was, and it suddenly felt important for him to keep her that way. *I can hold out one more day.* Lord Coventry was finalizing arrangements for their wedding ceremony that would take place tomorrow.

Yes, one more day.

"Tynan? The strawberries?"

He shook his head and laughed. "Yes, my love. Eat as many as you wish. Have them all. But let me help you dress first."

She regarded him with confusion. "You'd like me to dress? I... I don't have to." But the fiery blush on her cheeks spoke otherwise. "That is, if you have other intentions."

"Rest assured, my intentions are thoroughly dishonorable. I'm a wicked earl, after all. But I'm also about to be booted out of the club. I'll be a married man by this time tomorrow." He shook his head and sighed. "And I think that it is important to our marriage that you maintain no doubt about my reason for marrying you. So, even though I wish to bury myself in your lovely, rose-scented body, I think I shall find an empty bed of my own for the next few hours."

She nodded, but had a pouty curve to her lips that he found irresistible. "You're right, of course. You must think me wanton."

"No, my love. I just think you're beautiful." He crossed to her side in two strides and drew her into his arms. Her lush body responded to his touch, pressing to his hard planes and igniting a fire within him. He lowered his mouth to hers and kissed her with all the depth of his frustration.

She responded with equal fervor, clinging to his shoulders and twisting his shirt between her fingers as she savored the heated moment.

"I don't ever want to let you go, Abby." He tightened his hold on her, gently crushing her up against him.

"Then don't let go of me." Her voice was whisper soft. "I'd rather have you than those strawberries. Although they do look awfully delicious."

He chuckled again and eased away. "Indeed, I'm sure they are. But not nearly as tempting as you. I'll come by in a few hours to take you home. Tomorrow I will stand with you before the altar at St. Paul's Cathedral and pledge my heart to you. I love you, Abby. I never want you to have any doubt or ever feel shame with me."

THE FOLLOWING MORNING, Abby stood in front of the altar at St. Paul's Cathedral more certain than ever that she'd been blessed with a miracle. Not only was Tynan standing beside her looking wickedly handsome, but he also looked as though he had no second thoughts about taking her as his wife.

Her brother had surprised Tynan by eagerly giving his consent to their marriage. In truth, he'd thoroughly shocked Tynan, for he'd thought the worst of Peter until that very moment. He hadn't trusted Peter to do the right thing. Abby had worried as well. She knew her brother loved her, but feared the opium had destroyed every vestige of family love he'd ever held.

To her relief, one thing Peter did not have the strength to do was negotiate the terms of her betrothal contract. Not that it mattered. Tynan would have given him anything he asked for. Lord Coventry had stepped forward to act on behalf of Peter, feeling it was his duty to protect her.

Abby was up in arms that they were even negotiating terms. She wanted Tynan.

She did not care that he was an earl.

She did not care that he was wealthy.

She wanted *him*.

"Abby, having any regrets?" Tynan teased as their marriage ceremony was about to begin.

"No, my love. I fear you are stuck with me." She was barely able to contain her smile. The joy she felt was like a sunbeam lighting up the entire cathedral. But she did not know how to be any other way. She gave all of herself. This was her strength, but she also understood it was her aching vulnerability.

Tynan took hold of her hand, surprisingly elated for a man who was about to give up his bachelorhood. This meant he'd be giving up his quarters and membership in the Wicked Earls' Club. "I feel no remorse," he'd told her earlier. "I'm no shallow youth who knows nothing of the world. I've seen and done too much, in truth. Yet, these experiences have prepared me for this moment. I'll make myself available to Coventry should he ever need me, but there will be no more wild nights for me at the club... unless the woman I am bedding is you."

Abby looked forward to satisfying his needs in that regard. Their joining would be everything special. Passionate, tender. Meaningful. Filled with love.

"I do," Abby said in response to the archbishop's question, giving Tynan's hand a joyful squeeze.

Tynan responded with his 'I do" when asked the same question. "Yes, I will take Lady Abigail for better or for worse. I'll protect her always." He knew the qualities he wanted in a wife and declared aloud that Abby had them all. Strength of heart. Compassion and kindness. Beauty and intelligence.

"Tynan, I love you," she whispered when he bent to kiss her.

What would have happened had he met her a few years ago? Would he have fallen in love with her then? She hoped he would have. But at that time, he might not have done anything about it. Women like Lady Bascom and the marchioness would have lured him away.

She shook out of the thought as he led her down the steps from the altar and faced the ebullient horde that was his family rushing forward to congratulate them. Peter was not well enough to join their celebrations, but Abby had made certain to see him early this morning.

Tynan wrapped his arm around Abby's waist. "I love you, too. Brace yourself, the Braydens are about to descend on you."

Then she was out of his arms as Sophie and James hugged her to welcome her into the family. Tynan's mother, aunts, cousins, and most of all, his brothers, gave her their sincere well wishes. "So, the wolf has caught his rabbit," Ronan teased his brother as the three of them stood quietly aside while the rest of the family made their way out of the cathedral to Lord Coventry's residence where the wedding breakfast was to be held. "Or should I say, the little rabbit has caught her wolf?"

Tynan threw back his head and laughed. "Let's just say we caught each other."

Ronan looked from one to the other. "Any regrets?"

Tynan understood his brother was asking out of curiosity. He'd wondered the same about James when he'd married Sophie. "Not a one. You'll understand when you find the right girl. Her smile will slam into your chest and you'll be helpless to resist."

Ronan nodded thoughtfully.

"But don't go looking for love just yet," Tynan teasingly warned. "I need you to keep your mind on estate matters while I'm in Falmouth with Abby."

Ronan cast Abby a wincing smile. "It isn't much of a start for the two of you. Much of your time will be taken up with your brother, Abby."

Tynan replied for both of them. "It isn't traditional, but nothing about my courtship of Abby has been. I didn't even realize I was courting her. But her brother's recovery is important to her and that's what matters. Abby will fight as hard as she can to make it happen. She has me to help her now. She obviously has all of the Braydens in the palm of her hand and willing to help as well."

"Lord and Lady Coventry, too," Ronan remarked.

Tynan nodded and turned with a wink toward Abby. "They've practically adopted you as their daughter. I thought the buttons on Lord Coventry's vest would pop off, he was beaming and so puffed up with pride as he walked you down the aisle." He ran a hand raggedly through his hair. "But all jest aside, Abby. I'll move heaven and earth to make you happy, I want you to know that."

"I do know it, my love."

Ronan cuffed him on the shoulder. "Lord, when did you get so wise? You were always such an ass." Joshua and Finn had no idea what they'd just been talking about, but considered it their duty to cuff him as well.

"Boys!" Their mother's sharp rebuke carried halfway across the cathedral. Of course, they were among close family so she held nothing back in blistering her sons. Finally, she turned to Tynan. "Westcliff, you ought to be ashamed of yourself. You are neglecting your new wife."

Abby shook her head and laughed.

So did he.

They rode to Lord Coventry's home in the privacy of the Westcliff carriage, but they had little respite before they were crowded by relatives at the wedding breakfast. Every time Tynan approached Abby, someone steered her away. Every time she started toward Tynan, someone intercepted her.

Tynan, apparently feeling a similar frustration to hers, suddenly swept her into his arms and marched toward the door. He paused at the threshold. "I shall neglect my new wife no longer. A good evening to all."

It was barely two o'clock in the afternoon.

Finn was foolish enough to point it out and immediately received a cuff from their mother. "Be quiet, you foolscap."

Abby was blushing fiercely as Tynan called for his carriage. It was quickly brought around and within a few minutes they arrived at his townhouse. "Welcome home, Lady Westcliff."

Her heart was in her throat. "Thank you, Lord Westcliff."

He had a way of smiling at her that stole her breath away. He'd spoken to his brother about the power of a smile. His had captured her heart the moment she'd met him. It still had the power to enchant her. She was helpless to resist its charm.

He surprised her by opening the front door himself. "I've given my staff the day off. We have the house all to ourselves."

He lifted her into his arms again and carried her upstairs to his quarters. The room was decidedly masculine, his elegance and power reflected in the mahogany paneling and pine green drapes. His large, four-poster bed dominated the room and rested upon a maroon and green oriental patterned carpet. His writing desk was also of polished mahogany. Her rooms adjoined his, but she had yet to see them or the rest of the house. "I'll take you on a tour of your new home afterward. We have more pressing business to attend to first."

She was his now and he meant to make her so in every way.

Although his servants had been given the day off, they'd anticipated their needs and provided amply for them. Wine and refreshments had been set upon silver trays atop his writing desk. There was an enormous amount of food, enough to feed them for a week. They would never have to leave his bedchamber.

He put her down gently in the center of his bed. "Abby..."

"You needn't be polite or worried about my delicate sensibilities, Tynan. I don't think I have any when it comes to you. Nor am I hungry for anything but you," she admitted with a blush. "I'm glad you got the special license. I'm glad our wedding took place today. It was a beautiful affair and perfect in every way."

"So are you, my love." Her breath caught in her throat as he slipped the tea rose silk gown off her and then set it aside. His gaze was hot and fiery as he slid his hands along her exposed legs to remove her shoes and stockings.

She trembled with pleasure at his touch.

He had big, nicely formed hands, but they weren't those of a pampered lord. There was a slight roughness to them that heightened her pleasure as he slid them along her skin.

"I love the softness of your body and its subtle rose scent." He kissed the inside of her thigh, his intimate touch setting off fireworks throughout her body. Every part of her was in a frenzy of excitement. A thousand butterflies were flying amok in her belly.

He cast her a sensual smile and drew back to remove his own clothing.

She held her breath as he stripped off all but his trousers, and watched him with avid curiosity, barely able to concentrate for the hot tingles rampaging through her body.

His eyes were alight with the promise of passion.

He had looked as sinfully handsome on the night they'd first met, the taut muscles beneath his golden skin rippling in powerful waves along his solid arms and broad chest.

Mercy.

He returned to her side, his hands once more gentle and caressing on her body as he traced them over her hips, her breasts, and then over her shoulders to remove her delicate chemise. He took a deep breath as he studied her womanly splendor, and then released a stream of air with a strained groan. "Abby, you're so beautiful."

He said no more as he unpinned her auburn hair and ran his fingers lightly through the long strands, allowing them to tumble in a soft cascade over her shoulders.

No man had ever touched her like this. She suddenly felt embarrassed, for she wore nothing but her modesty.

But he was a wicked earl and had no such modesty.

Nor did he wish to hide himself from her.

She looked her fill. Her feelings had been stripped bare from the moment she'd met Tynan and now her body was as well. But she trusted him. With her heart. With her happiness. With their marriage. He removed his trousers and turned to her so that his every sinew and muscle was revealed.

"Abby, let me guide you. I won't hurt you." He kissed her softly on the mouth and then settled beside her on his bed. She sat up with the sheet covering her chest. Her shoulders were bare, her skin a pale pink in contrast to her vivid auburn curls spilling over them.

She reached out to him, knowing he would be especially gentle with her this first time.

He slipped under the covers and rolled her under him, his gaze hot and seductive as the weight of his body intimately pressed against hers. "I love you, Tynan," she said and lost herself in the majestic power of his touch.

He was heat and hard strength and muscled, golden skin.

Then he was fully atop her, propped on one elbow while his hands stroked over her body and stirred the flames of her already heightened desire.

The weight of him felt reassuring. "I'll be here for you, Abby. Always."

She ran her hands over the taut, rippled planes of his body. She arched and moaned and closed her eyes to experience each euphoric sensation roused by his hands and mouth on her hot, tingling skin.

She opened all of herself to him.

He caressed her intimately with his fingers, probing the most sensitive spot between her thighs until she was a liquid pool of fire. He closed his mouth over her breast, teasing and suckling its sensitive peak until she could no longer contain herself and cried out in fervent ecstasy.

"Move with me, my love," he said, entering her with a gentleness she never imagined possible. He took her passionate cries into his mouth, kissing her and making her feel so truly loved, so truly joined. One heart. One body.

Then his cries matched hers and they soared together for a long, splendid moment, like two majestic birds floating among the clouds. He held her closely, their damp bodies in a hopeless tangle between the sheets as they slowly drifted to ground, panting and laughing and both of them feeling quite fulfilled.

"Tynan, dear heaven. Is it always like this?" Her heart was hammering in her chest.

Her bones had turned to pudding.

She couldn't stand on her own two legs if she tried.

But she didn't have to stand alone anymore. She didn't have to face Falmouth and her brother's problems on her own. Tynan would be standing by her side.

"It will always be with you, my love." He trailed light kisses along her throat, his manner comforting as well as arousing. He shifted her in his arms so that her body rested atop his, the heat and magnificent power of his body exciting her again. The subtle scent of roses – her scent – mingled with his masculine sandalwood scent. The sensation of his hot skin and the golden hairs across his chest felt divine against her cheek. "How do you feel, my love?"

She purred contentedly. "Like a very wicked countess."

"Ah, but that will not do. This earl has given up his wicked ways."

"Not all of them, I hope."

"Not all." He kissed the throbbing pulse at the base of her throat, and then grinned naughtily as he rolled her onto her back and settled over her, the weight of him intimate and exquisite. "I still have the peacock feather."

"Hurrah!" She cheered again and kissed him soundly on the lips. "I shall finally find out what all the fuss is about."

He laughed. "I love you, Abby."

They slept little that night, but when the first light of dawn filtered in from the window, Abby awoke in Tynan's arms. She was Lady Westcliff now, well and truly. She was no longer alone and overburdened. She had Tynan to stand beside her now. Sunlight fell across his handsome face and illuminated his golden hair. She snuggled against him. "I love you, my wicked earl."

He gave a sleepy chuckle. "I love you, my beautiful rabbit."

He rolled her under him and took exquisite care in showing her just how much.

THE END

Dear Friends,

I hope you enjoyed Earl of Westcliff, and if you did, then please consider leaving a review for it on your retail outlet. It is most appreciated! Now, I'd like to introduce you to a few more Regency earls in this Wicked Earls' Club series, as well as Tynan Brayden's cousin, James Brayden, whose story is book 1 in my The Braydens series. James is the Earl of Exmoor, the wounded warrior hero in A Match Made In Duty. When he agrees to marry the sister of a dying comrade in arms, he never expects that this favor will turn out to be his salvation. James has a broken and battle-scarred heart in desperate need of healing, and Sophie Wilkinson is just the heroine to heal him. There will be more Braydens to come, because these big, brawny Braydens are talking in my head, and Ronan, Romulus, Finn, and Joshua are all demanding their stories.

Read on for an excerpt of A Match Made In Duty.

Happy reading,

Meara

A MATCH MADE IN DUTY
CHAPTER 1

London, England
October 1815

JAMES BRAYDEN, FIFTH Earl of Exmoor, glanced at the bottle of brandy his butler had just carried in on a sparkling silver tray and set down beside him on the elegant mahogany desk in his study. He waited for his butler to depart and close the door behind him before turning to the two guests who had just arrived and were about to change his life forever. "Care for a drink, Major Allworthy?"

Ordinarily, he would have given his friend, Lawrence Allworthy, an amiable pat on the back and poured them both a tall glass of the fiery amber liquid his butler had just brought in. Ordinarily, they would have settled in the cushioned leather chairs beside the blazing fire and spent the night getting drunk while reminiscing about the men in their regiment and the years spent on the Continent battling Napoleon's forces. Ordinarily, their first order of business would have been to toast their fallen companions.

But tonight was no ordinary night. His gaze settled on the young woman with lustrous dark hair and big, brown eyes who stood quietly beside his friend. "And you, Miss Wilkinson. May I offer you tea? Refreshments? The journey could not have been an easy one for you."

"No, thank you." She blushed as she spoke and then looked down at her toes, obviously wishing to be anywhere but in his study.

James decided the rose blush was quite becoming on her cheeks.

He leaned on his cane to slowly walk around the sturdy desk that dominated the center of the room and came to stand beside his guests. Up close, he could see that the young woman was trembling, though she did her best to hide her fear as he approached. Were his scars so hideous? He supposed they were, for even he had yet to grow used to them. They'd be most alarming to a stranger. "Please," James said, motioning to the chairs beside the fireplace. "This will be your home soon, Miss Wilkinson. You may as well get used to it."

She pinched her lips and frowned lightly. "I don't wish to be rude, Lord Exmoor. But what makes you think I wish to accept your proposal?"

He exchanged glances with Lawrence who appeared as surprised by her remark as he was. "It was your brother's dying request that I marry you. I promised him that I would and I intend to honor that vow."

Her pink blush deepened. "Do I have no say in the matter?" She tipped her chin up to meet his gaze, and although she was small and slender, the top of her head barely reaching his shoulder, he could see that she had a full-sized, stubborn determination.

Lawrence cleared his throat. "Miss Wilkinson, what choice do you have? Do you not wish to marry an earl? I do not know of any young woman in your circumstances who would refuse—"

"Major Allworthy," James said, quietly interrupting him. "I think it is best that I speak on my behalf." He understood the young lady's reluctance now that she'd taken a good look at him, and expected that she was now quietly swallowing her revulsion. While his leg would hopefully strengthen in time, the jagged scars etched on his face were permanent and unfortunately, too prominent to hide. "No doubt the terms of our arrangement must concern you. We ought to go over them now, for you may have some misconceptions about what... ah, I shall expect in your duties as my wife."

He raked a hand through his hair. "Perhaps we ought to speak about this matter in private. Major Allworthy... Lawrence, would you mind giving us a moment alone?"

His friend appeared to be as uncomfortable as James was and more than eager to leave this embarrassing discussion to him. "Excellent idea. I'll be in your library. I'm sure there's a book I'm eager to read." He dashed out as though his coattails were on fire.

The girl appeared desperate to follow him out, but James placed a light hand on her elbow to hold her back. "Give me a moment of your time, Miss Wilkinson. Hear me out before you walk out of here." He cast her a wry smile. "Or run out. I wouldn't blame you."

She relented with a curt nod.

"Please, let's sit beside the warming fire." He settled her in one of the chairs and took the other. She must have noticed the awkward way he sank into the soft maroon leather and stretched his leg in front of him since he could not yet bend it. But she said nothing, and to her credit, made no moue of distaste.

"I know this isn't easy for you," he said, uncertain how one politely raised the issue of the bedchamber to a young woman one had known for all of two minutes. Yet, that particularly thorny issue had to be foremost on her mind and James knew he had to address it immediately. "Rest assured that I will not... er..." *Bloody humiliating!* In all his days, he never imagined himself in this awkward situation. Before the war, he had been considered quite the catch. Beautiful young women threw themselves in his path with tedious regularity, all of them eager to gain his notice in the hope they might become the next Countess Exmoor.

Now, they darted away in the hope of avoiding him. All but the most desperate and browbeaten debutantes whose families were in dire need of funds to maintain their estates. He ran a hand across the back of his neck in consternation. "I promised your brother I would take care of you. He extracted my promise to marry you, for he feared your cousin would not be generous with you once he took title to your brother's holdings. His fears obviously proved correct. What would you have done had Major Allworthy and his wife not been at hand to bring you to London?"

Her face began to heat and he knew it had nothing to do with the heat of the flames burning in the hearth. "I would have managed, my lord. I am not your charity case."

"Indeed, you are not."

"My lord," she said more insistently as she met his gaze. "I agreed to accompany Major Allworthy in the hope that you might help me find suitable employment."

He arched an eyebrow. "You're asking me to renege on my promise to your brother?" In truth, he liked that directness about her and the fact that she did not flinch when looking at him. "I cannot do it, Miss Wilkinson. I'm offering to make you my wife. In truth, I'd be honored if you accepted. I know I'm rather a poor specimen."

She quirked a soft eyebrow in what appeared to be surprise. Was she disputing the obvious? "Certainly not the husband you might have hoped for," he continued, "but you will always be safe here and treated with honor." He cleared his throat. "You shall have your own bedchamber, of course. And I shall not impose on you."

Lord! How much plainer could he state that he'd keep his hands off her?

Her only response was a slight widening of her big, chocolate brown eyes, so he continued the uncomfortable conversation. "I am under no illusions. The war took its toll on all of us. Whatever hopes or dreams I may have had…" He motioned toward his face. "Well, I'm no longer any woman's idea of perfection."

Her lips turned upward in the hint of a smile. "My lord, may I be impertinent?"

He much preferred it to her being a timid mouse around him. "Of course."

"You seem to think I'm a simple-brained ninny and that my only requirement in a husband is a man with a pretty face. I assure you, I am not that shallow." She let out a soft sigh and leaned closer so that he caught the subtle scent of lavender soap along her slender throat. "I will not deny that my situation is dire. But that does not give me the right to interfere with your future happiness. As you can see, I have little polish. I'm no society gem." She shook her head and sighed again. "How can you possibly think to make me your countess? I'm a penniless stranger with no family connections."

"I gave your brother my word and I intend to keep it. I would do the same if you had the face of a wart hog or the brain of a goose. Thankfully, you have neither of those qualities. All I ask is that you live under my roof – separate quarters, of course – and act as my hostess when the need arises for me to entertain at home. I would also ask that you accompany me to the balls and other social engagements to which we shall be invited."

She tipped her head and nibbled her lip as she studied him, her gaze once again direct and assessing. "A business arrangement."

"Yes." He nodded. "You shall have an allowance, of course. Your days will be mostly your own."

"I see." She stood and had the courtesy to pretend to study the flames brightly glowing in the hearth while he struggled to his feet in order to stand beside her. "I suppose we ought to shake hands to seal our bargain."

Was she accepting his terms?

She stuck out her small, gloved hand to confirm it.

He wasn't used to shaking hands with a woman, for those of his acquaintance merely dangled their fingers before him in expectation that he would bow over them and mutter some polite inanity. But Miss Wilkinson, although quite genteel in her looks and manners, had a no nonsense way about her. He set his cane aside and swallowed her hand in both of his. "Done."

He expected a trumpet fanfare. A chorus of angels singing. A tremor along the ground, for the prospect of marriage was no small matter. But all was silent. Even Miss Wilkinson was holding her breath, no doubt contemplating the bargain she'd just made. "One small request," he said, still holding her hand and noting that she'd made no move to slip it out of his grasp. "In public, I shall call you Lady Exmoor. But I'd hoped for something less formal when we are alone at home. What is your given name?"

She laughed lightly and shook her head. "Did my brother neglect to mention it?"

James cast her a wincing smile. "He mentioned it a time or two, but more often he referred to you as… Smidge."

She couldn't help but laugh again, but that melodic trill was punctuated with a groan. "Oh, dear! That was the awful pet name he gave me when we were children. I hope you will banish it from your memory at once! My name is Sophie."

"Sophie," he repeated softly. "Nice to meet you. I'm James."

END

Want to read more of A MATCH MADE IN DUTY? Go here:
books2read.com/matchmadeinduty

ABOUT THE AUTHOR

Meara Platt is a USA Today bestselling author and an award winning, Amazon UK All-star. Her favorite place in all the world is England's Lake District, which may not come as a surprise since many of her stories are set in that idyllic landscape, including her Romance Writers of America Golden Heart award winning story, Garden of Dragons, released as Book 3 in her paranormal romance Dark Gardens series. If you'd like to learn more about the ancient Fae prophecy that is about to unfold in the Dark Gardens series, as well as Meara's lighthearted, international bestselling Regency romances in the Farthingale Series (Laurel's story, A Midsummer's Kiss, is the 2017 RONE award winner for best Regency romance), please visit Meara's website at www.mearaplatt.com.

57425195R00067